P9-APX-721

SOMEBODY,
PLEASE TELL ME
WHO I AM

HARRY MAZER
and
PETER LERANGIS

SOMEBODY,
PLEASE TELL ME
WHO I AM

SCHOLASTIC INC.

ACKNOWLEDGMENTS

With thanks to Steven Sabella

This book is a work of fiction. Any references to historical events, real people, or real locales are used fictitiously. Other names, characters, places, and incidents are products of the author's imagination, and any resemblance to actual events or locales or persons, living or dead, is entirely coincidental.

No part of this publication may be reproduced, stored in a retrieval system, or transmitted in any form or by any means, electronic, mechanical, photocopying, recording, or otherwise, without written permission of the publisher. For information regarding permission, write to Simon & Schuster Books for Young Readers, an imprint of Simon & Schuster Children's Publishing Division, 1230 Avenue of the Americas, New York, NY 10020.

ISBN 978-0-545-56637-7

Copyright © 2012 by Harry Mazer and Peter Lerangis. All rights reserved. Published by Scholastic Inc., 557 Broadway, New York, NY 10012, by arrangement with Simon & Schuster Books for Young Readers, Simon & Schuster Children's Publishing Division. SCHOLASTIC and associated logos are trademarks and/or registered trademarks of Scholastic Inc.

12 11 10 9 8 7 6 5 4 3 2 1   13 14 15 16 17 18/0

Printed in the U.S.A.   40

First Scholastic printing, January 2013

Book design by Laurent Linn
The text for this book is set in Augustal.

For Norma

BEFORE

May 5

The knife came out of nowhere.

Ben Bright sprang back. His arm knocked the weapon into the shadows and nearly clocked his best friend, Niko Petropoulos.

"Nervous, are we?" Niko said.

Ben felt his heart race. His best friend was Sharked up, his hair slicked back and a cigarette pack rolled in his sleeve. Up close he looked ridiculous, and on a normal day Ben would have laughed in his face.

But not today. Today he wanted to shove Niko through the curtain. Or weep. Instead, the two impulses met in the middle and canceled each other out, and he said, "You scared me."

"That makes two of us. Look what you did." Niko lifted his shirt, revealing an ugly, purplish bruise. "I would like you to stab me again. And do it right this time."

The bruise looked like a piece of steak or a great big rotten cabbage. Or the map of a distant, dead planet. "I did that?" Ben said.

"At dress rehearsal. You had your finger hooked around the blade, so it didn't retract." Niko was staring at him strangely. He lowered his shirt and leaned forward, raising an eyebrow. "What's up?"

"Nothing," Ben lied.

"You look like you're about to pass out, or get sick. Which is okay. Nerves are normal. People hurl on opening nights, all the time. Just don't do it here. You've already abused me enough. You're graduating. I've got another year for humiliation."

"I don't have to hurl. I'm okay."

"Ladies and gentlemen." Niko pantomimed holding a mike. "Tonight. *West Side Story*. Eastport High School, New York. A performance that redefines Method acting—Tony actually *kills* Bernardo. Casting for replacement. Must be unbelievably buff and own a Kevlar vest. Details at eleven."

Now everyone was staring: The sophomore playing Riff. Three Latino cast members practicing the Mambo. The weird little wardrobe kid who smelled like wet shoes. Which just made Ben feel worse. He hated keeping secrets. He hated doing things without telling anybody. He had to make it through this day, just this day. He could tell people tomorrow.

For now, he wanted to freeze time. To photograph them all and hold this moment tight, so he could retrieve it a month from now. So he could feel everything—the opening-night mania, the way Niko's comments made him tongue-tied and unclever, the curve of his girlfriend Ariela's back as she stretched at the barre. The way everyone shut up and paid attention whenever he appeared onstage. All the stuff he would be leaving behind.

He spun and trapped Niko in a headlock. "I'm a spaz, okay? I don't belong on the same stage as you."

"Murder!" Niko cried. He jerked loose, shaking his finger. "This is your inferiority complex. It makes you passive-aggressive. Or just aggressive. You need someone to convince you, for the trillionth time, that you're God's gift to the theater. Oy. Someone, please get him a Tony Award before he kills me!"

"Save the award, I'm getting the plastic knife," Ben said, turning away.

That didn't make sense. Everything out of his mouth felt *off*, like a bad taste. He walked carefully, threading through the squealers and warm-ups and grim line-reciters. His knife would be somewhere among the thicket of legs.

"Be-e-e-ennnyyyyy!" Wendy Leff enveloped Ben in a massive hug. Justin Milstein jumped in on the action, too, then Sarah Welch. The entire cluster nearly collided with Ariela Cruz, who was sitting on the floor near the back wall.

"Unhand the Wonk," Ariela said. She was in a full split, leaning over a show poster she'd just signed.

Ben gently pushed aside his friends. "You're my hero," he said. "But . . . Wonk?"

"I have this new theory," she said matter-of-factly. "There are three types of people who do theater. Type One is the Needies." She waggled her fingers at Wendy. "They're in it for the love and hugging. Two is the Bloviators, who get off on the attention. That would be cough cough, Niko, cough. And Three is the Wonks, like me and you, the process junkies. Acting, singing—we just like doing it. It's a *good* Wonkness."

A shrill voice pierced through the noise, "Half hour,

please! Half hour!" Jeannie Lin, their stage manager, wound her way through the crowd, clutching a clipboard. Seeing Ben, she held out a tired-looking plastic knife and recited in her same announcer-voice, "And hold on to your props, people!"

Ariela smiled at her as she marched away. "I hate when she calls us 'people.'"

"Me too," Ben said. "'Lords and Ladies' would work just fine."

"Ha." Ariela held out the poster, with a Sharpie balanced on top. "This is a present for Ms. Moglia. Sign under my name, okay? So Tony and Maria will always be together." She batted her eyes with an irony that felt somehow comforting at a time like this.

Ariela's name was huge and bold, with a heart sign over the *i* and a gushy, theater-y message, but Ben signed only his name in quick, tiny scribble.

"Modesty, in a guy, is so hot," Ariela said with a sigh.

"I suck! I so totally suck!" Niko's voice eagerly piped up from behind Ben. "At everything."

"Modesty," Ariela said, "not idiocy."

"Look what your modest boyfriend did to me," Niko said.

Ben could tell by Ariela's nose crinkle that Niko had lifted his shirt again.

"He's gentler with me. Well, mostly," Ariela said. Standing up, she handed Niko the poster. "See if you can find room for your whole, long Greek name. Or just write 'Douchebag.' It's shorter. And pass it on when you're done."

With a sly wink at Niko, she gave Ben a kiss and moved to an emptier spot at the barre. "Don't say anything," Ben murmured.

"You mean, like, 'Lucky bastard'?" Niko said. "Okay, I'll just think it."

"Compliment accepted. I think."

"So, have you guys set a date?"

"Just sign the poster."

Niko leaned in closer. "I'm serious. We've talked about this—"

"Hypothetically. And in private."

"Nobody's listening. I find the idea fascinating." Niko carefully signed his full name, Nikolaos Dimitrios Petropoulos. "You and Ariela . . . settling down, getting married, auditioning, living together in some rat-infested love nest in Brooklyn . . . down the block from me and Taylor Swift."

Ben was in no mood for Niko's predictable unpredictability. "Later, okay? She's going to be in Ohio next year. And you know it. If you want to rehearse, come find me."

He began walking away to look for a quieter, less annoying spot.

"And you? Where are you going? How come you never talk about that?" Niko barreled on, following close behind. "I mean, you and Ariela have been together since you were in diapers, you still love each other's asses, and you both know you couldn't do better. So . . . you wouldn't do anything stupid to screw that up. Am I right?"

Ben whirled around. "If this is some kind of nut-job acting exercise, it's over. Now let's do the scene or go back into your hole."

Niko had a weird look. Ben knew the look. Sometimes

when Niko wanted something, he didn't give you the pleasure of stating it outright if he could make you guess it.

"Are you jealous?" Ben said with exasperation. "Is that what this is all about? Can you hold it in until after the show?"

"Come at me." Niko struck his fight pose. "Come on, Tony, you greasy slimebag, Polish gringo. Come and get Bernardo, the brother of your sexy true love."

"Twist my arm." Making sure to grip the knife with the handle only, Ben lunged at him. Niko flew back, just as rehearsed, and Ben lunged again. He aimed away from the bruise, a couple of inches closer to Niko's midsection, and plunged the knife inward. He could feel the blade retracting smoothly into the hilt on a spring. He'd done it right this time. Niko was supposed to flex his torso and freeze for a moment, letting the audience see that he'd been stabbed. But instead, he grabbed Ben's arm and flipped him to the floor.

"Hey!" Ben shouted.

Niko was on top of him, pinning him to the dust-covered floorboards. Which was unfair because Niko wrestled varsity.

Ben forced a laugh. "Okay, okay, we're even. Let go."

"Not yet," Niko said, his voice a raspy whisper. He leaned closer, his eyes narrowed and angry. "You got your notice, didn't you?"

Ben felt himself grow suddenly cold and numb. "*What?*"

"You don't want to say anything because it's opening night," Niko said. "Right? Because you're such a friggin' modest Boy Scout. Because you're so *It's not about me.*"

"Asshole." Ben struggled but couldn't move.

"I know what you did. Tell me the truth. Because there are only two things that could make you act so weird. One is that Ariela is pregnant—so it must be the other thing."

"You're freaking crazy."

"Crazy but not stupid. If I'm wrong, say it. Say 'You're wrong.' Just those words."

Ben lurched forward, ramming his forehead into Niko's brow.

As his best friend fell back with a yowl, Jeannie came running toward them. "Guys! What are you doing?"

Ben forced a smile. "Just rehearsing."

"Nice move." Niko rubbed his head. His eyes had changed, as if a cloud front had moved across them. "It'll come in handy with the ragheads."

"Don't use that word," Ben snapped.

"You can tell them, 'Hey, terrorists, it's not about *you*.' Teach them the Gospel of Ben and save the world from Islamists."

"Um, you guys? We're almost at fifteen—" Jeannie said.

"*We know, okay?*" Ben snapped. "*Go away.*"

As she huffed off, Niko glanced over toward Ariela. "Have you told her? I'm sure she'll be okay with the fact that you're giving her up. Not to mention your friends and your future. To join the freaking Army and fight a war we never should have gotten into! And Chris. What's he going to think? Did you ever think about the fact that your brother needs you more than the Republican party does?"

"It's not a party, it's a country," Ben said. "And I'm not

going anywhere but boot camp. Just because you and everyone else in this school aren't doing what I'm doing, doesn't make you all right and me wrong."

"You want to know what's wrong? It's wrong to waste talent. It's wrong to keep it from the rest of the world. It's selfish."

"There are thousands of people who can act and sing."

"There are thousands of people who can take a bullet for no good reason."

Do. Not. Let. Him. Get. To. You.

"Fifteen minutes, people!" Jeannie shouted. "Fifteen!"

Ben stood calmly. "I need to get ready. Do you want to do the scene again?"

Niko looked at him dully and turned away. "Break a leg, Private Bright. And crack a skull while you're at it."

2

Ben wasn't feeling in the mood to eat or party, even though (1) the revolving Lazy Susan at Lily Hong's was practically cracking with the weight of the feast, and (2) Ms. Hong had allowed him to blast his own playlist over the speakers.

He wanted the night to be over. Ariela was dancing with a bunch of Jets and Sharks girls, most of them still in their makeup. After too many attempts to bring Ben into their circle with a magnetic glance, she had given up. Niko hadn't spoken to him except as Bernardo on stage, and the anger in the fight scene had been scary good.

Ben watched his mom and dad try to carry on a conversation with the Gleasons, whose older son had served in Desert Storm. They all looked very intense.

Ben felt a tap on his shoulder. "Squash court. Locked door. An ax, a baseball, a whip, and a can of Diet Coke. Tom Seaver and Slobodan Miloševieć". Who lives?"

Chris was looking at him expectantly. "Squash court?" Ben asked.

"An enclosed environment," Chris explained. "Thirty-two feet long by twenty-one feet wide by eighteen feet high. They can't leave until one of them dies."

Ben thought a moment. "Well, Seaver has a stronger arm but Milošević" is nastier . . ."

"Want to place odds?" Chris asked.

Out of the corner of his eye, Ben spotted Ms. Moglia gesturing toward him from another table. Chris was already sitting and drawing some elaborate diagrams on the tablecloth. "Three to two odds, Seaver," Ben said. "Although I think I'll regret it."

Chris nodded. "Oh, yes, you will." He held up his right hand stiffly.

Ben slapped it. "Da man, brother!"

"Da man," Chris said.

Ben walked over to Ms. Moglia's table and slid into the seat next to her. She offered him a steaming plate of shrimp with Mala sauce, but he shook her off. She looked at him slyly. "'Smatter, don't you like Szechuan dishes?"

Ben smiled. "They's all right, I guess."

"You're sharp," she said with a surprised cackle. "Okay, details."

"*Lady Sings the Blues*," Ben replied. "Billy Dee Williams and Diana Ross, playing Billie Holliday."

"Original line?"

"'Smatter, don't you like . . . ' some flower. Gardenias?"

"Smart *and* talented!" She put her hand on his arm. "And lucky. I have some news for you. Come."

She stood up and headed for the nearby wall, looking over her shoulder as she evaded waiters and dancing patrons. The wall was flooded with crisscrossing lights in different shades of red and amber, and she turned to face him under a dragon-shaped wall sconce. "Okay, *entre nous*," she said in an exaggerated stage whisper. "You know I hate to brag, but when I was at Northwestern I dated David Ashman." The last two words were spoken in the reverential hush befitting a Hollywood director.

"You've only told us that about once a week in class," Ben said.

Ms. Moglia gave her own cheek a theatrical slap. "Motormouth. Well, I Friended him last month and, lo and behold, he accepted. Okay. Are you sitting down? No, you're not, because there are no seats. No matter. He's not only the hottest young player in TV—well, young-ish—but, drum roll, he's casting a new teen TV show. Are you ready for this? Musical theater high-school kids."

"Sounds familiar."

"Well, yada yada, a new twist, whatever," Ms. Moglia said. "Point is, he's in the NYC area. What do you think would be the chance I'd get him to come to see a high-school show? Zero, under normal circumstances—in other words, if he hadn't just happened to be looking for teen talent . . . " She paused dramatically.

"So . . . what are you saying? He was in the audience?"

"Not only was he," Ms. Moglia said, "but he asked about you."

Ben laughed. "Why, did I spit on him?"

"*Oy*, you are so self-effacing I almost can't see you." She grabbed Ben by both shoulders, and from the look on her face it may have been to keep herself from flying away. "*He said you were good. Which means he may want to see you for the show!*"

Ben felt a momentary rush. It was hard not to be swept up in the enthusiasm. But Ms. Moglia was a dreamer. She had "made it to the final cut" of a dozen Broadway shows, been "singled out" by every famous director alive, and would be a huge star today if not for finances/backstabbing/sickness/misunderstanding/her own refusal to compromise quality.

She was a kickass drama teacher and a lovable person, but a grain of salt was required.

"Great," Ben said. "Maybe I'll get a screen test someday."

"I have a message in to him right now about that very thing." She smiled knowingly. "To think I will have known you when. Don't forget me in your Oscar speech."

"I'll let you write it for me."

"Done."

Ben turned to see Ariela waving at them. He waved back. He felt sweat beading on his forehead. Ms. Moglia was so happy, and he wanted to feel happy too. This was supposed to be a great night. The show had gotten a standing ovation, he hadn't cracked on the high note in "Maria," he hadn't murdered Niko, and a famous director had witnessed his triumph. The music, the lights, the food, and Ms. Moglia's news would make any normal person proud of himself. He tried.

Ms. Moglia sighed. "Your reaction is noticeably muted."

"Yeah," Ben said. "Sorry."

"Muted is not in the palette of emotions I would have predicted. What's up, honey? You can tell me. Why?"

He thought for a moment. What the hell. Everybody was

going to know sooner or later, especially now that Niko knew. "Well, you might feel a little muted too if you were leaving for boot camp after graduation."

"Say what?" Ms. Moglia said.

"Muted but excited, I mean," Ben said. "It's a privilege and opportunity, too, but on a different scale. Though not much chance to sing and dance, I guess."

She gave him a sidelong glance. "Joke. Okay. You got me. I'm just a little gullible."

"I'm serious," Ben said.

"Yeah, and I'm Ethel Merman." Ms. Moglia tossed back her head and laughed. "Now go dance with that hot chick who's been staring at you all night before she burns a hole in the back of your head. And tell her the good news."

Ariela had run out of the restaurant barefoot and was halfway across the parking lot with a notion to walk all the way home, when Ben had found her and talked her into his car, where she was now sitting, a shoeless prisoner.

"Are you warm enough?" he asked.

She couldn't unclench her jaw to muster an answer. He had been yammering away with Ms. Moglia when Niko Petropoulos had sprung the news on her. And now here she was, trapped, driving into a parking lot at Jones Beach like a nighttime hookup in the dunes, and all she wanted to do was walk into the surf and keep going.

"Okay," he said as he pulled into a parking spot. "If you're not going to talk, at least listen to me."

"You are an idiot," she said, climbing out of the car. "Everything positive I have ever said about you, every word, I take back. How could you do this? How could you *think* of doing this? Tell me this is a joke, Ben. Tell me this is something Niko made up. Because if it is, I'm going to kill him. And if it isn't, I'm going to kill you."

He was standing on the other side of the car now, his eyes brimming. "I wasn't going to say anything. I was going to let you have the night."

"'*Let me have the night*?' What is that supposed to mean? You were going to humor me, let me bask unknowing in the innocent glow of this, the pinnacle of my high school career—all the while you and that jackass Niko are pitying me, laughing behind my back at my ignorance! And then what—tomorrow morning you call me? 'Hey, later, Ariela, I'm going to war. You were killer as Maria!'"

"No!" Ben said. "It wasn't like that! And I'm not going to war!"

Ariela turned her back. Looking at his face upset her too much. She began walking toward the ocean. The waves were calm, washing into the shore with confident little slaps. A couple of sandpipers followed the edge of the backwash, and a seagull swooped down loudly, making off with a Skittles wrapper. She could hear Ben padding behind her. He was a sensible guy to the last, and he was going to let her have some space. That was his modus operandi—do whatever the hell he felt like, and then let everyone else reel while he waited. "Don't follow me," she said.

"I'm your ride," he replied.

"I can get home by myself."

"It's eleven miles."

"I know how to take a bus."

"They don't run at this hour."

"I'll sleep here. I'll float out to sea. I'll keep walking until I reach Far Rockaway. And then Manhattan. And then Omaha."

She felt his arm touching her waist. "Please. Let me talk to you."

Ariela spun around. A tear was making its way down Ben's right cheek, or maybe it was just condensation. She felt short of breath. "Why?" she said, fighting to keep the anger that despite her better judgment was dispersing like spindrift into the salty air. "Why did you do this without telling anyone?"

"I knew you would all say I shouldn't do it. And I knew I had to do it. I didn't want the conflict to wreck the rehearsal period. So I figured I would just wait." He shrugged. "It was stupid, I know. Selfish."

She looked into his soft, expressive face. She could identify every emotion that was washing over it, one by one—he was embarrassed, resolute, wronged, sympathetic, protective, confused, afraid. As much as she hated him this minute, he amazed her. As she had watched other guys morph painfully into creaky, pimplified approximations of manhood, Ben had slid by them, arriving there quietly without losing the softness of a boy. "It's not selfish, Ben. Not what you just agreed to. It's the opposite. It's masochistic. It's saying you're not worth anything. All your talent, all your brainpower, just give it to the

U. S. and let some faceless jackass with a blackmarket AK-47— "

"I'm not going to war!" Ben said. "I'm volunteering for the reserve. I've been thinking about this all my life. You're the one who always says *be different*. Well, do we know anyone who is going to serve? No. Ninety-nine percent of our friends are going off to college, and then what? Finance? Law? Banking? That's not a waste? People like us *should* volunteer—kids with privilege and skills and talent. So-called. I want to reach the end of my life and say, 'I did something important. I saved lives.' My grandfather was a prisoner of war, and he is the strongest, kindest, most accomplished man I know."

"He would have been even if he didn't serve," Ariela snapped back. "And what makes you think *you* wouldn't do something important if you didn't go? Think about it, Ben. Your grandfather had to serve. He had no choice back then. In this century there are *always* people who'll want to join the Army. But you have amazing things to give the world *now*. Why wait?"

"Singing? Acting? There are always people who'll want to do that, too. The world will get along fine waiting for me to return."

Ariela felt a migraine coming on. The air was suddenly way too cold, and the screeching of the seagulls was getting on her nerves. She turned away, not willing to let him have the satisfaction of seeing her disintegrate.

"Maybe the world can wait," she said, heading back toward the parking lot. "But I'm not so sure I can."

3

Letter left by Ben Bright on June 21 upon his departure for basic training in Fort Benning, in an envelope on his bedroom desk and marked DO NOT OPEN UNTIL AFTER I LEAVE.

Dear Mom, Dad, and Chris,

You have been amazing to me these last few weeks. Very respectful. Thank you for not screaming and making feel like a moron. But I know you're keeping stuff inside, and so am I. I suck at speaking up and explaining myself, so I hope you don't mind me doing it here. It's kind of chicken of me, I know. Basically if I write it down instead of saying it, I don't have to see you crying.

I know how you guys feel about the war. Dad, you especially, with what happened to Uncle Brian in Vietnam. But believe it or not, that's one factor in my decision. Also 9/11. I know I was a kid then. But Mom, you still talk about watching the news about Kent State when you were a girl. How they killed those innocent kids and how it scared you and stuck in your mind and shaped you as a grown-up. Same thing. And Dad, you talk about how as a defense attorney sometimes you have to represent people you think are total dirtbags. But you do it with all your heart and skill, because it's your job to make the system work for ALL the accused. Because "only through a robust and honest legal system, with dedicated and competent professionals, can there be justice." Your words.

I think of both of those things all the time. I understand all the politics. I know the U.S. could have responded in different ways back in 2001, etc. But I still dream about those buildings, and the people who were inside them. Who had no choice and no chance. When jumping 100 stories is the better of two options to a person who's done nothing wrong, that's more than injustice. That's a country under siege by thugs. I still think defense is an important part of what makes democracy work, just like you do, Dad. And it needs dedicated and competent professionals.

Like the person I'm about to become.

I love you, and Gram and Gramps and Papa and Nana and Chris, more than I can say. I'm doing this so my kids and their kids can have the freedom to say the same things to me.

Love,
Ben

P.S. Chris, I'm counting on you to keep me up on the Mets this season. I want to know everything.

P.P.S. Hold on to the other two envelopes I've enclosed — the one that says Do Not Open (that's yours) and the other that says To Ariela. I'll take them back when I get home. Open them if I don't. Sounds morbid, I know. Don't worry, you know me, drama at any cost. Please take care of her while I'm gone. No matter what happens. In my life or hers.

4

"I'm proud of you."

Ben had not expected that from the mouth of Ariela Cruz. She had waited till the last minute, till they were standing on the platform of the Long Island Rail Road station next to Ben's overpacked duffel bag, while both their families sat tactfully in the waiting room.

It sure made what he had been gathering the courage to tell her a heck of a lot easier. "Really? Proud?" he replied. "Can I unlock my knees now? I was prepared for you to push me onto the tracks."

"That's not funny," Ariela said. "That's not even close to funny."

"Sorry. I'm just shocked. And glad." After weeks of arguments, explanations, political discussions, crying, near-break-ups, and truces, this was the first time she expressed anything more than a grudging understanding. "But . . . really? Why?"

Ariela took his arm. "I guess I think you're brave. And the military is lucky to have you. And that even if the other soldiers are, like, ten percent as good as you, the country's in excellent hands. I think that I'm sorry I've been so awful to you. I think I love you. And I think I better shut up before I totally make an ass of myself."

She buried her head in Ben's down coat. Her shoulders began to heave gently, rhythmically. He held her tight. He'd always felt lucky to have her in his life. He knew he would be way too lucky if she were still in it by the time he returned. He was determined to do everything in his power to make that happen.

And for the three thousandth time, he followed this chain of reasoning to conclude he was an idiot for agreeing to do this instead of going to college. Life would have been so much easier.

He told himself for the three thousand and first time that college would be there when he returned. The country was full of kids filling seats at colleges of their choice, but not so many willing to fight for the society that made those choices possible. He believed this deeply, but he'd learned the hard way not to announce it to too many others because it tended either to make people glaze over with false bravado or spit out scripted-sounding antiwar screeds.

"Promise me one thing," Ben said. "No matter what happens, you'll stay in college and finish."

"Duh. You thought I was going to sit around like Penelope and wait for you?"

Ben hip-checked her, gently and away from the tracks. "Seriously. When I leave, you're going to start feeling all guilty. From those people who tell you that you should be going to New York and audition before you get too old. College is a really good investment."

"Thanks, Dad." Ariela grinned. "You promise *me* one thing.

When you get back, you'll go to college too. So I can outrank you because I'll be a year ahead."

"Deal," Ben said.

"And take this with you," Ariela said solemnly, pulling an oblong box from her pocket, "so you'll always remember what you're fighting for."

Ben felt his eyes moisten. He opened the box carefully, unwrapped the neatly folded tissue, and pulled out the plastic retractable knife from *West Side Story*.

"Yeah, yeah, I know, call me sentimental," Ariela said.

Ben laughed. But there was something else rattling inside the box. A silver chain with a simple locket. He pulled it out and sprang the locket open.

Inside was a photo Ariela had taken, of the two of them at Jones Beach.

He put the chain around his neck and tucked it into his shirt. "Thanks," he said. This was it, the moment. If he let it pass he might never have the guts to do it again. "I have something for you, too."

He pulled out a Cartier box that represented five years of mowing lawns, babysitting, homework tutoring, selling stuff on eBay, and a couple of magazine print jobs and TV spots. Not to mention a substantial loan from Mom and Dad, who were reluctant about the idea at first but gave in when he enlisted.

"Oh my god," Ariela said.

"I know, it's a cliché, right?" Ben said. "I'm marching off, the train is coming in—"

"I wasn't thinking that at all." She wiped a tear from her

face and carefully opened the box. In the dullness of the overcast morning, the diamond looked less impressive than it had at the store.

"What were you thinking?" he asked.

She was crying now. "I was thinking yes."

Then he kissed her, as the 7:14 to Penn Station barreled in.

5

Email received by Ariela Cruz, July 19:

FROM: US ARMY
TO: ARIELA CRUZ
hey! cant take a lot of time so pls forgiove
mistakes . well just as we kinda expected we r
gonna be deployed. its not too bad tho b/c if yr
going to pick an area of iraq this one is relatively
safe. the lt is this guy named nails (it has nothign
to do with maincures hahaha) actualy hes
supposedly the best in the military at ,aking
friend s w/ the hajjis (that's the name we call
iraqis, after the muslim hadj(and they say its like
mr rogers neighborhood. i told them i was glad it
wasnt peewees playhouse but they didnt get the
joke. so dont wory ok? i will c u very very soon
w/ lots of cool stories to tell already i have some
I cant print here!

xoxoxoxxoxoxox,

u know who

ps. pls tell mom & dad & chris the news. i wrote
earlier today but wew hadnt got the deployment
orders at that time. tell chris we have a yankees
fan here his name is mendez but everyone
calls him da bronx. for about a week i had him
convinced i was derek jeters 2nd cousin. dont
know why i did that, maybe b/c YANKEE FANS
ARE SO GULLIBLE!!!!

Niko was mowing the Brights' lawn when Ariela arrived. Only
she didn't much resemble Ariela but some pale zombie replacement. He cut the engine and ran over to greet her. "You okay?"
he asked.

She held up a printout. It was wrinkled and then smoothed
out again, like she had thrown it out and then recovered it.
He read it carefully and felt his stomach jounce. "Oh, crap,"
he said.

Ariela nodded. She opened her mouth to say something,
thought better of it, and then just shook her head.

Niko reeled as he read it a second time. He'd had nightmares about this since Ben had left.

I'm not going to war. How many times had Ben said that? Of
course he was going. They all went. They went and came back,
and then they went again and again, until they were used up
and scared and too shattered ever to return. And then they
were sent back again.

He couldn't believe the tone of it. Like the whole thing
was a big party. And the misspellings and clumsy typing, as if

he had regressed, as if they had taken the man and turned him back into a kid.

"Did he at least cc his mom and dad?" Niko asked.

"Doesn't look like it," Ariela whispered.

"What the heck was he thinking?" Niko rubbed his forehead. Ben couldn't have been so stupid, so callous as to write only Ariela and expect her to be the messenger. Then again, he'd been doing a lot of stupid things lately. "We'll go in and tell them together."

Ariela looked away, then let out an enormous, shaky sigh. "Niko?" she said.

"Yeah?"

"What are we going to do?"

He opened his arms, and she sank into them, her own arms limp by her side. She began to sob—wracking, shaking moans that scared him. "We're going to be here for him, that's what."

The words sounded hollow and trite as they came out of his mouth, so he just shut up and held her, both of them rocking, both of them sobbing in full view of the neighborhood as a distant lawn mower *yaa-yaahed* loudly, like a cruel laugh.

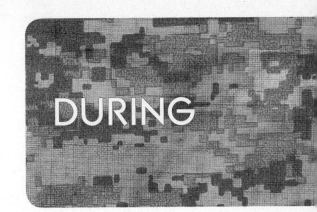

DURING

September 15

The explosion came at 07:13:00 a.m., when Charlie Company had been out of the wire maybe ten minutes.

At 07:12:23, Ben Bright was walking beside a Humvee, eight measures into "Something's Coming" from *West Side Story*. If memory served his company leader right, it was the part that went "It may come cannonballin' down from the sky," ironically enough.

During boot camp, Ben hadn't had the guts or the energy to sing. He'd only started at a Camp Idol karaoke night, and only after lots of encouragement. But once he'd started, there was no stopping, even after the deployment orders.

That was where he'd gotten the nickname Broadway. Not very imaginative, but then none of the names were, really. Bolcomb from Arkansas was Hayseed. Mendez from Fordham Road was Da Bronx. Reiner, who looked like Schwarzenegger before he got fat, was Governator. And Katrina Westhof was Catwoman.

Ben liked his name. It reminded him of who he was and what he was going back to. It reminded him of Ariela, of her yes on the platform of the Long Island Rail Road. Yes to a ring that wouldn't be paid up for another few years.

Yes was what had been getting him through. Singing kept

yes alive. And on a mission through the Iraqi desert, where heat and silence were like solid things, people wanted songs.

Especially people forced to walk beside the vehicle because troops on foot look "friendlier."

The blast, which came out of nowhere, seemed to rip the voice out of his throat.

He dropped to the road like dead weight. Beside him, the Humvee jolted. In a nanosecond, an instantaneous flip-book of odd memories flashed through his brain: Ariela in her sea-green halter top, Dad yanking a bluefish from the Montauk riptide, Niko and Ben racing down Atlantic Avenue after stealing a comic book from Howie's, Mom crying after *West Side Story* ...

Then, a dull metallic thump, and the images stopped.

Ben hacked on the sand, which had caked into his face and seeped between his teeth. His eyes hurt as they opened. The road stretched out, coated with sand and leading to a small collection of sand-colored buildings just ahead. He smelled sweat and garbage. Either they had survived, or heaven was just like Iraq.

Spectacles, testicles, wallet, watch. All accounted for.

The Humvee was intact, too. The thump had been courtesy of a very angry Private Wade "Hayseed" Bolcomb, who had hit his fist against its side door. "Where'd you get your license, Mendez?" he yelled. "Wal-Mart?"

From the Humvee's passenger seat, Devon Johnson was howling. "Da Brrrronnnnnx!" he shouted. "Yo, Mendez, you ever heard of a Wal-Mart? They got Wal-marts in Da

Brrrronnnnnx? Today only! Driver's licenses, faw f'r-a dolla!"

"Yo, Broadway, you got any songs about loser New Yorkers who never learned to drive?" Hayseed asked.

So that was it: Raoul Mendez had backfired the engine, which sounded like a bomb blast, and now the guys were giddy. You had to be, when your life passed before your eyes and it was just a mistake.

"Shouldn't have taken off the training wheels!" came a shout from the other side of the vehicle. It was either Hideki or Governator. They sounded the same, although one was skinny as a post and the other could have been a body double in *Terminator*.

In the gun mount, Catwoman held her head in her hands. She was from outside Keokuk, Iowa, and the best shot Ben had ever seen. "You want to switch places, Bronx?" she called out. "My daddy taught me to drive on a tractor. I can handle this."

Ben couldn't see Mendez in the driver's seat. But he heard a whole bunch of words peppered with the phrase "your mother."

"Dang, look at this crap," Hayseed drawled. A cloud of sand billowed around him as he wiped himself off. He was the biggest of the unit, maybe six six, with a drawl so thick you first thought he was from some foreign country. Or planet. "And here I was, all ready to show off my pretty new uniform to the Hadji girls."

"Maybe they have a Laundromat in town," Ben said. "Then you could prance your junk around while you wait."

"You're the prancer, Broadway. Me, I'm the dasher. And I

get the vixens! Yes! Yes! Am I a po-wet or what?" Hayseed tried to hide a self-satisfied smile but couldn't. He spat. "Frickin' sand. Makes me think of my mama."

The Humvee was moving again, its treads digging into the cracked cement road. Ben shouldered his rifle and began walking. "Okay, I'll bite. How is the sand like your mama?"

Hayseed nodded, falling in beside him. "I could blow up half of Iraq and eat the children for lunch, I could become a billionaire selling plutonium to Iran on the black market, I could steal the life savings and the clothes off the back of Muhammad in that house over there, and my mama would organize a damn pig roast for all of Jonesboro when I got home. But if I tracked this crap into the house, *wham!*—out on my butt. She's the one that made me so OCD. Know what that is? Obsessive Compulsive Dickhead." He spat out a line of sand onto the ground. "What's this stuff made of anyway?"

"Soil. Rock. Dust." Ben hocked a lungful off to one side. "Hey, know what dust is? Mostly dead skin. I read that somewhere."

"And you think this hick is stupid enough to believe that."

"Never said you were stupid, Jethro."

Hayseed gave a sudden lurch to the side, nearly knocking Ben off his feet. "Sorry, must be the Tourette's," he said.

Ben was cracking up. "Tourette's, OCD . . . what the hell else do you have?"

"I'll tell you what I have, is a friggin' driver's license," Hayseed said, glancing toward the Humvee. "*He* don't, you know. Bronx."

"Serious?" Ben said. "Does Nails know?"

"Mendez says they don't teach you to drive in the Bronx. So Nails decides we're his teachers. The Bronx Remedial Driving School, Hadji Division. Says they ain't no better way to learn how to drive."

"And get us all killed," Ben said.

"I know, right? Don't make no sense."

Through Ben's sunglasses, the village loomed larger. The heat swirled up from the sand and pavement in tight little eddies. Tiny figures, clad in loose-fitting white clothes, were stopping in their tracks, staring balefully.

Everyone talked about Embracing the Suck. The Suck began at basic training, which broke you so that only the strongest could come out the other side. Then you received your deployment, and Suck now equaled Fear plus Loathing. Then your first few weeks in Kuwait, waiting for orders, and a convoy into Iraq across the desert. Suck to the suckth. But this—meeting the people you were here to help, right in their homes, and knowing that they hated your guts—this was Suck Unembraceable.

They were scared and angry. They couldn't see what you saw—schools for girls, power plants, crops, construction, new markets, real freedom. They had no electricity or running water, practically no medical care, and the Sunnis breathing down their backs. You were a pack of well-fed infidel kids, armed to the gills and looking for insurgents. If there was one hint of one Al Qaeda there—one poison apple—then everybody suffered.

You are after their hearts and minds . . .

That was what Lieutenant Leonard "Nails" Nelson had

drummed into their brains. Nails was known for his ability to gain trust among the locals. Supposedly this is what had kept the troops alive for three months, not a single casualty. Publicly, everyone respected that.

Nails also called the current mission Operation BFF. Privately, they all thought he was a little nuts.

"Look at them," Hayseed said under his breath as he glanced around. "They hate us."

"We must be like outer space men," Ben said.

"Operation BFF, Big Friggin' Fools," Hayseed drawled. "Where's our fearless leader anyway? Back at FOB looking at Internet porn."

"He's entertaining some major," Ben said.

Hayseed raised an eyebrow. "Like I said."

The locals began slinking back into their houses. They moved like wisps of smoke. Ben fought to keep from shaking. He recited Nails's words to himself: *Face-to-face contact makes human connection. It's their country. We have to act like guests— guests whose job is to protect and defend them. Which means men on the ground, gifts, playing with the kids.*

It also, apparently, meant using a Humvee driver who grew up in the only place in the U. S. where people didn't get a driver's license at age seventeen.

He wondered what Nails would think if he actually *saw* Mendez's driving. Ben glanced at the vehicle nervously. Bucking a bit, slowing and speeding, heading unsteadily into town. Into the thicket of diverted eyes, untreated illnesses, and hunched backs.

"Ready to be a hero?" Hayseed asked.

"With pickles and mayo," Ben replied.

He remembered the last thing his pastor, Father Joachim of the Eastport United Church of Christ, had said on the day he left home. "May God be in your back pocket."

The Humvee bucked. Mendez cursed. Johnson stuck his head out the window, pretending to be carsick.

Ben thought, *May God be in the carburetor, too.*

7

In a moment the Humvee roared into the village. Despite the migration indoors, the town center was still packed—men in groups talking animatedly, women hanging out with kids, older kids playing unrecognizable games in the sand. At the soldiers' approach, their eyes seemed to glow through a scrim of sand, their expressions ranging from impassive to hostile.

"Wave to the Hadjis," Hayseed said. He nodded amiably at an emaciated white-bearded man in front of a clay shack, who was so still you couldn't be sure if he was alive. "Hey, Shep, how 'bout them Texas Rangers? Nice lawn you got there! Can I borrow your weed whacker? How 'bout borrowin' your daughter? What'zat? Can't tell 'em apart? Oh well, my loss. Catch you next time. Happy birthday!"

The man's eyes glimmered slightly. He broke into a smile and waved back.

Whatever crap comes out of your mouths, keep it low, and eyes off the women, Nails had said. "Dude, maybe he knows English," Ben whispered.

"Maybe he's got a daughter," Hayseed said, casting a deceptively respectful glance at three middle-aged women in hijabs, who were carrying small sacks over their shoulders. "Ooooh, dang, my knickers are in a twist over that one."

"Which one?" Ben asked.

"The one with the beard. Well, the lightest beard."

"Guess I got the one with the nose," Ben said.

"You'll never need a can opener, Abdul."

"They got cans here?"

"Hey, she's looking at you. Don't look back, she *is*. Sing to her—go ahead, Broadway! No show tunes, though, please. Maybe some Eminem. You know who that is?"

Suddenly, Catwoman's voice pierced the heat. *"Eleven o'clock! Eleven o'clock!"*

Hayseed fell silent. Ben felt the hairs rising inside his helmet, neck to crown. The road ahead curved to the left. Maybe fifty yards. Through the heat's haze, Ben spotted something by the side of the road. A shapeless, sand-colored lump.

"Canvas sack! Canvas sack!" Hideki shouted.

Mendez braked. The Humvee lurched, then stopped. Johnson wasn't laughing.

Ben dropped to his knees. Trash was the enemy in Iraq. Trash, bumps in the road, potholes, anything that could hide an IED.

Instinctively he raised his rifle. He scanned the area for suspicious movement, men with metal objects in their hands. Cell-phone signals activated IEDs. The guys would wait till the vehicle ran over the item. The bombs were homemade, stuffed with nails and metal scraps for maximum damage. The force of a well-timed blast could rip apart the heavy armored Humvee like a tuna can. It could shred a human body.

Ben's heart seemed to slow. The world around him was

suddenly clearer, sharper. He was vaguely aware of families all around him moving, oddly organized, like choreography. He saw the old man's robe disappear into a doorway. An arm dragging a crying kid behind a house. In a moment the street was empty, as if the people had just dissolved into the sand.

"*Wires, Big G?*" Johnson.

"*Negative.*" Governator. With high-power binocs.

"*I got the jammer activated.*" Mendez. Nobody making fun of him now.

Then Ben stiffened. On the second floor of a long, stucco building to the left, he saw a man, bald and middle-aged, wearing a striped shirt and clutching a cell phone. "*TEN O'CLOCK! TEN O'CLOCK!*" Ben shouted, running toward the building.

Hideki was beside him, rifle pointed.

"*WINDOW. SECOND FLOOR!*" Hayseed.

They were moving toward the building, but also closer to the canvas sack. At some point, you would be too close. Ben thought about Mendez and the infrared jammer. It didn't always work.

The bald guy was shouting something now, something with the word Allah in it. Everything they shouted seemed to have Allah in it. A bullet ricocheted off the wall, two inches from the window. Hideki was firing.

Ben saw the man's silhouette passing through another window, followed by two other men.

Three more shots, maybe four. He crouched, shielded behind a post, and took aim.

"*Move! Move! Move!*"

Governator raced to the door of the building and kicked. It ripped off its hinges, and he burst in, rifle first. Hideki followed, taking position.

Catwoman called out, "*Heads up!*" She was in the Hummer, still in the gun mount.

Ben could hear a shot. A volley of shots came from behind them. Pieces of the building's upper walls exploded in puffs of cement debris.

"Come on!" Hayseed shouted, racing to the door.

Ben felt his feet moving. He was in the building now, in the darkness and the stink. Hideki and Big G were racing upstairs, followed by Johnson. But the building was long, and the guy could come down into a section even closer to the sack. He could be luring them. This could be some kind of suicide mission.

No. If it was, they'd be wearing the explosives, he thought. But he didn't believe it.

"*Moving below!*" Ben shouted, hugging close to the first-floor walls, swinging the rifle left and right, with Hayseed and Mendez behind.

They surrounded the bottom of another stairwell. Boots clomped overhead, past their location. To their right, a closed door. Ben kicked it down and moved in. A woman shrieked, arms stretched toward him, pleading. On the floor was a tiny ancient man, his face like a skull.

No. It wasn't an old man but a kid—a teenager, so sick and wrinkly he looked about seventy-five years old.

"We won't hurt you!" Ben shouted, knowing they wouldn't

understand his words but might pick up his meaning. "We're not here for you!"

There was a huge clatter in the next room. Hayseed was in first. Hideki, Big G, and Johnson were racing down the stairs and out a back door. The end of the building.

Somehow the guy and his pals had escaped.

Ben followed them out, into the sun's glare. The three men were streaking across the desert in sandals, their white garments flowing like gull's wings. Ben eyed the sack. It was thirty, forty yards away, but the men were out of range. "*Let's get 'em!*" Hayseed shouted.

"No!" Johnson said. "In the Humvee! Everybody!"

Hayseed's eyes were crazy-wide, his teeth clenched. Back home, he had some sort of state high-school record in kickoff returns and, fully armored, he could do the hundred meter in twelve five. "I could take them bastards," he murmured, his voice choked with frustration.

With a grunt that seemed to come from his toes, he pulled a grenade from his belt, turned to the building, reached for the pin.

"Stop!" Ben shouted. He ran in front of him, hands in the air. "There's a mother in there, dude, with a sick kid!"

"*Hayseed! Broadway!*" Johnson shouted. "*In the Humvee. Now!*"

Hayseed lowered his arm, turned from Ben, and spat into the dust. "Where's my engraved invitation?" he growled as he strutted toward the vehicle.

Ben ran ahead and pulled open the Humvee door. With its armor, the thing weighed four hundred pounds.

"Back it up, Bronx!" Johnson was shouting. "And follow the Yellow Brick Road home. Around Hadjiville!"

Mendez jerked the Humvee into reverse. Then he turned and took a wide berth around the two clay shacks, which were now deserted.

No. There was a kid, a little girl in a ripped white smock, standing petrified in the shadow of the last house. In the pathway of the Humvee was a small, stuffed red doll.

Tickle Me Elmo.

Ben remembered. Hayseed had given it to the kid just last week. It was a gift from a Sunday school in a Tennessee church. Now it was splayed out in the sand, and the little girl who left it there was too scared to fetch it. Mendez swerved.

Catwoman was steady in the mount, her rifle pointed across the desert. "Got the Three Stooges in sight!" she shouted.

The Humvee shook with her machine-gun fire. Maybe one hundred fifty yards away, one of the men dropped. "*Straighten out! Straight! That wasn't our guy!*" she bellowed.

Ben could feel the Humvee accelerate. The child was staring now, but not at the toy. She was fixing the men in her gaze as if trying to record their faces, her eyes a luminous, steely blue.

Behind her, a wiry boy stepped out of a door. Maybe twelve years old. He thrust his hand forward, shaking. In it was a sliver of metal.

Ben felt a fist clutch his heart.

"*The toy!*" he shouted. "*THE TOY!*"

It was the last thing he said before the Humvee rolled over Elmo.

8

September 15

At 07:43:48:25:07, a shaky finger presses send.

A signal reaches a hidden cell phone. The phone detonates a small mortar shell packed with screws, nails, and bolts.

The ground explodes in a hailstorm of dirt and rock. The phone is instantly pulverized. The force upends a four-ton armored vehicle like a toy truck. The metal debris penetrates much of what was left intact.

The heat incinerates the flesh of soldiers protected by Kevlar helmets, ceramic-shell Kevlar vests, and thick boots. A wave of superheated, extreme high pressure instantaneously boomerangs to extreme low.

Human tissue violently contracts and expands. The sturdiest structures, bone and flesh, fare the best. But blood bubbles, eardrums snap, hearts go into shock.

Brains fold inward on themselves and then billow outward, soft as trapped jellyfish. The precise electrochemical connections short-circuit—connections that control thought, smell, taste, touch, sight, sound, movement, memory. Connections that define what it means to be human.

In a millisecond, that definition changes.

And, at 07:43:48:25:08, so does the life of Benjamin Bright.

AFTER

9

September 16

"When did it happen?" Mrs. Bright said into the phone.

"What?" her husband said. "What happened? *Put it on speaker!*"

Niko fought to stay upright. They were all cleaning up after a late summer barbecue, a celebration of Chris's fifteenth birthday, when the call had come in.

Mrs. Bright fumbled with the phone for a moment, and then a tinny voice blared out:

" . . . medevaced him with several of the other boys immediately after the incident, where emergency care was given en route to Baghdad . . . "

Oh god, oh god, oh god. Niko had had nightmares about this very thing. Ben's tank running over a mine. He had made the mistake of uploading *The Hurt Locker*, even though Ariela had told him he was crazy to do it. "Is . . . is he . . . ?" Niko said.

Mrs. Bright nodded and gave him a thumbs-up. Leaning toward the phone, she said loudly, "And what's his condition now?"

"Stable," the voice replied. "The tank shielded him from serious physical damage. Some shrapnel in both legs, but no loss of limbs, no severe internal tissue wounds. The size and proximity of the blast, however, has put him into a temporary coma. There are preliminary signs of TBI, but those are to be expected."

"TBI?" Mrs. Bright said.

Chris, who had been manipulating a Rubik's Cube that someone had given him, piped up, "Traumatic Brain Injury. Ben has Traumatic Brain Injury."

"Yes, that's correct," the voice replied. "Forgive me for not explaining that, Ma'am—"

"There are three different scales to measure traumatic brain injury," Chris said. "There's the Glasgow Coma Scale—"

"Ssh, not now, Chris!" Mr. Bright said, then turned back to the phone. "When do you expect him to regain consciousness?"

"Unclear, Sir," came the reply. "It will take some time to know the extent of the damage."

"You just said there was no damage!" Ben's dad blurted out. His face was bone-white, his eyes wide and hollow-looking.

"In situations such as this," the tinny voice continued, "there may be a degree of memory loss, mood swing, severe headaches. With bleeding, there is risk of certain kinds of stroke. Encroachment on the cranial nerves could affect eye movement, muscle control, touch, and smell. Things of that nature."

"Things of that nature," Mr. Bright murmured.

"Where is he now?" his wife asked.

"Landstuhl, Germany, at the moment, sir," the voice answered. "He is safe and breathing well. We believe Benjamin is stable enough to fly to Walter Reed tomorrow or the day after. Can there be someone there to meet him?"

"You bet your four-star ass," Mr. Bright said.

His wife gave him a sharp look. "Thank you so much, Captain. We will be there."

10

September 16

Ariela hated waking up after one o'clock p.m. It meant you might not make it from the dorm to Prince in time for lunch, and you were stuck with having to pay somewhere else or starve until dinner. Plus, it was a Sunday and she had planned for a marathon session at the library to work on a paper that was due the next day, and she was ripped at herself for partying so late last night. Not to mention the fact that, upon her return, she had to sleep on the common room sofa because her roommate Kate had a guy in their bedroom, with whom she argued until five a.m.

Rushing to get out of the room, she was in no mood to receive a text from Niko. "Leave me alone," she murmured, setting her phone to vibrate and sliding it into her backpack. She leaned into her mirror and fixed her unruly mountain of bed-hair.

"I take it that wasn't your boyfriend," said Suzanne, her other, less volatile roommate, who was from Vermont and woke up with perfect straight hair every day, not that there was any causal relationship.

"I wish," Ariela replied, swinging her pack over her shoulder. "It's his best friend."

"Yeah? What's he look like?"

Ariela laughed. "You don't want to know. He's been a

mess since Ben left. He's more worried about him than I am. And that's saying a lot."

Before leaving, she adjusted her ring snugly. It had become too big over the last month, a reminder that she'd lost ten pounds since arriving at Chase College. The insomnia and lack of appetite had taken their toll. It was abnormal to lose weight during freshman year, her envious friends never ceased to tell her. But it was also abnormal to have a fiancé, let alone a fiancé who happened to be in a war. Everybody was pretty cool about it; they asked all the right questions and didn't look at her like she was some kind of simpering war bride. But still, it would have been nice to have one friend who knew what this felt like.

Suzanne was ready now, so they both barged out of the suite and rushed down the corridor. In the bathroom someone was gargling aloud to a blasting iPod dock. They went down the stairs and out the front door, into a warm September afternoon.

"Is he gay?" Suzanne asked.

"Ben?" Ariela replied. "I hope not."

"No! The best friend!"

"Just a little compulsive. Plus he's still a high-school senior, so he's near Ben's family, and all the reminders. . . . "

They crossed the street and turned right onto Center Path. This was Ariela's favorite part of Chase, a gentle gravel/dirt path that bisected the campus and served as a gathering place for students. She liked the sense of comfort and familiarity here. Even though she'd only been in college a month, she already knew pretty much all the faces.

"Have you heard from him lately?" Suzanne asked.

"Niko?" Ariela said. "All the time."

"No, your boyfriend. Fiancé. Whatever."

Ariela sighed. "Not really. He can't write a lot. The web-cam doesn't work, and they can't really use the phone. So it has to be e-mail. And even that's not great, because everyone has to line up, so there's pressure to finish, and everyone's looking over your shoulder. It sucks."

"Sext him, baby," Suzanne said. "Let the whole base get off."

"Oh god, you're giving me naughty ideas."

"Ah, well, at least there's no competition, right?" Suzanne said. "As they say, 'no horizontal mazurka with a lady who's wearing a burkha.'"

"Did you just make that up?" Ariela asked.

"Speaking of horizontal mazurka . . . " Suzanne was looking over her shoulder at a tall, tired-looking guy who was lurching across Mather Avenue. "Oh, Colter, make me happy," she said under her breath.

"That's a name? Colter?" Ariela said.

"Yes. And even though he looks like that, he's rumored to be smart. And god, can he sing. You should come to the a cappella meeting tonight. I'm trying out for the Creeks. We could be in it together."

"Will you stop?" Ariela said. It was about the ninetieth time Suzanne had bugged her about that topic. A cappella was not theater, and Ariela was way more interested in that.

"You are such a purist," Suzanne said.

Ariela's phone vibrated again but she ignored it. They were

passing through the stone gate into the main part of campus now. Some of the trees were already changing color. The sun glinted against the glass expanse of the art building, and the black crow statues on the roof of Hansom Hall seemed about to fly away.

She imagined Ben walking with her. He would love this place, she thought, but it would be small for him. With his talents, he'd probably be better off at a big university or a state school. Preferably one nearby. "Does Ohio State have a big theater department?" she asked.

"Huge," Suzanne replied. "If you like impersonal universities where people live and breathe football and speak in charming grunts. Why? You thinking of transferring already?"

"Just asking. For Ben."

"Tell him to come here. We can share him."

As they veered off to Prince, Suzanne's phone chirped. She quickly fished it out of her shoulder bag and made a face at the screen. "Five one six area code?" she muttered.

"Long Island," Ariela said. "My neck of the woods. Answer. You may have won a trip for two to Lake Ronkonkoma."

"Is that a real place?"

"Must be. I hear it on the train announcements."

"Hello? . . . *Who?*" Suzanne held out the phone, stared at it, and held it out to Ariela. "Weird. It's for you. Niko?"

Ariela threw up her hands. "How does he know your number?"

"He must really like you."

"He's being a pain in the butt. Can you take it? Tell him

I can't talk now. I'm being waterboarded as a sorority ritual."

Suzanne raised an eyebrow. "I charge for answering service duties, five hundred a minute."

"Okay, okay." Ariela grabbed the phone. "Make it quick, Niko. I'm in the middle of lunch and the rats are descending on my tray."

"I asked at student housing," Niko's voice said. It sounded distant and bloodless.

"What?" Ariela said.

"That's how I knew about Suzanne. You were ignoring me, so I called them and asked who your roommate was."

"And they just gave you her number, just like that—to a total stranger? Are we in a time warp?"

"They wouldn't, until I told them it was an emergency, and you were Ben's fiancée," Niko said.

Ariela stopped in her tracks. It felt as if background and foreground had suddenly merged, so she was seeing everything with equal focus: a squirrel's mad dash up a tree, a security cart nearly colliding with a skateboarder, a guy in a blue T-shirt juggling three oranges, the clock on her phone clicking to 1:27. As if the intensity would somehow slow time, would prevent Niko from continuing. "What emergency?"

"You need to come home, Ariela."

"Why?" she replied. "Tell me why, Niko."

"Just . . . come home."

"I'm five hundred miles away, I can't just come home!" She tried desperately not to raise her voice. She didn't think she was raising her voice. But now Suzanne was looking at her in horror. "Tell me what happened. Where is Ben? Is he all right?"

"No," Niko said. "No, he's not. He's been hurt. And we're all going to Washington to see him. There's a flight out of Columbus at 6:45, American Airlines. I can pick you up at Washington National. We already reserved the ticket."

Ariela let her arm droop. She mumbled a reply but the sound seemed to be coming from somewhere else. She felt Suzanne taking the phone from her hand. She heard her say something to Niko and then good-bye.

Then she saw nothing except the cool grass beneath her as she sank to her knees.

September 17

"He smiled."

"Well, I don't think so . . . "

"He heard my voice, and he smiled!"

"I think it was a reflex."

"Gas."

"What?"

"That's what we always said when he was a baby. He's not smiling, it's just gas."

"Right. Right. I remember that. Right."

"He's not a baby. He knows we're here."

"He looks so cold. Should we get the nurse?"

"How long before he's normal?"

"He is normal!"

"The doctor *said*—maybe a couple of weeks, depends on the tests."

"What kinds of tests? What are they going to do to him?"

"They say this kind of injury is unpredictable, Ariela. He had minimal penetration—"

"No bullets or shrapnel to the head."

"Right. That can cause the most overt damage. But this is TBI, traumatic brain injury. He's lucky to be alive."

"Is he going to be conscious again?"

"They think so."

"Because he's already missed, like, eleven Mets games."

"Well, you can tell him all about them, Chris. When he wakes up."

"Can I bring the newspaper next time?"

"Of course."

"He really doesn't look so bad."

"The hair will grow back, right?"

"He looks lumpy and weird. I mean, not *weird* . . . "

"He looks so peaceful."

"Oh, there, Ariela, don't cry. Look at him. Imagine how happy he'll be to see you."

"Do you think he'll be normal in time for his b-b-birthday? So we can celebrate?"

"That's five months away—he'll be running the marathon by then."

"And making his Broadway debut."

"He hears us, I know it! I can tell."

"Hey, bud. Do you know you're a hero? Do you know that we love you?"

"The Mets swept the last series in St. Louis, four to nothing, three to two, and nine to eight in eleven innings. They came back from four runs down, with a grand slam in the bottom of the ninth!"

"Does he have a radio? Maybe we can turn it on for the games."

"Right, Ben? You can hear?"

Noises and voices. Hear. Yes. Voices loud.

"We all love you, bud. We're so glad you're home. Hey, we

spoke to Lieutenant Nelson. He says you were among the best he ever saw—"

"*Are.* You *are.*"

"—and you're going to be decorated for your bravery, too. Okay. Hey. Anyhoo, they're gonna chase us out. We'll be back tomorrow morning, okay?"

"Chris is bringing a radio!"

"The newspaper, too. I'll read you the sports section! The Reds had a perfect game. The chances of a perfect game occurring are one in one hundred fourteen thousand."

"Did you feel that, sweetie? That was from Ariela, on your left side, and here's one from me, mommy."

Hurt. Scratch. Bad. Stop.

"We have to meet with the doctor now, but we'll be in the next room."

"Bye."

Sleep.

September 17

Niko fidgeted with this cell phone, even though it was off. The small briefing room made him feel claustrophobic and he didn't like looking at Doctor Parini.

She was nice enough. Friendly. Actually fairly cute, for a thirty-something doctor. That was the point, really, the perfect makeup and put-together hairstyle. It made everything strange and unpleasant. The measured voice and steady glance as she talked about Ben's "condition." Saintly. The class valedictorian all prepped for a blind date. You couldn't help but feel you had to thank her.

So nice of you to take the time out of your busy schedule to tell me how my best friend went to Iraq and came back a vegetable.

Mr. and Mrs. Bright were raw-eyed and looked about ten years older. Ben's brother Chris was peppering the doc with Chris-questions. She was sizing Chris up, her face uncertain and analytical for a moment, then suddenly snapping into an expression of composed competence. She had probably assessed his "condition" too, pinpointing his place on the autism spectrum to the exact decimal. Ariela had been calm, almost emotionless, when he'd picked her up at National, but from the moment she stepped into the hospital she'd been clutching his hand. She had a killer grip and he'd had to pry her loose, but now he wished he hadn't. That pain was preferable to this.

"Imagine you're in a familiar place," Doctor Parini said. "You've been there a million times. Then, one day, there's a blinding snowstorm."

"Sand," said Ben's little brother, Chris, tapping his foot and gazing around the room.

"Pardon?" she said.

"Christopher, please," Mrs. Bright said gently.

"There's no snow in Iraq," Chris said. "Just sand. That's what Ben wrote in his e-mail."

"It's a semaphore," his dad said.

"Metaphor," Mrs. Bright corrected him.

"That's what I meant," her husband said. "God, I'm losing it."

"Okay, good point, Chris," Dr. Parini said. "Sandstorm. So all of a sudden, sky and earth seem to merge. The landscape you know so well? It's blocked from view, just this wall of snow . . . er, sand. You see little pieces of the landscape peeking out—there! and there!—but they disappear just as fast. A little corner reminds you of a building. A window reminds you of a house, a wheel reminds you of a bike. The problem is, they're just hints of things you once recognized instantly. But they're hidden from you and you're disoriented. So you can't be sure of anything. What you think is a bike is a car. What you think is a school is a house. Everything is an impression, but it's not exact. So you move ahead, but you're no longer in control of what you know. You want to react, to say something, but—"

"But you wouldn't," Chris snapped.

"Wouldn't . . . what?" Dr. Parini looked at her watch.

"Move ahead," Chris said. "If it's a sandstorm, you have sand in your eyes and you'd be crying. Also cringing on the ground, because of the pain."

Ariela covered her face. Her shoulders started to heave. Niko put his arm around her and immediately felt awkward.

"I guess what I'm trying to say, Chris," Dr. Parini said with a patient smile, "is that along with his shrapnel wounds, Ben has had what we call a traumatic brain injury. We have a few ways of measuring how serious it is, but we will need more time to determine that. Most likely his neural connections have been disturbed, and the results can be unpredictable. There may be problems with his senses—touch, smell, sight, and such. He may require physical therapy to do the simplest things, like keeping his balance or even speaking. We should also be prepared for possible memory loss. He may not recognize you for a while, or he may think you're someone else."

"Like stuff in a sandstorm," Chris said, "that you can't recognize."

"Exactly," Dr. Parini answered. "The thing is, he may have thoughts, memories, but they will be like a code that he can't crack for a while. Some part of his brain will be manufacturing memories from his past, but another part will prevent him from expressing them—or even processing them."

"I can teach him the names of all the New York Mets, and their batting averages and even slugging percentages, I think, all the way back to 1962, when they were an expansion team,"

Chris said. "Well, maybe not slugging percentages." He began rocking and humming.

Niko recognized the tune. It was the "Meet the Mets" theme, Chris's favorite song. He would blurt it out whenever he felt stressed, even in public—especially in public. Ben was the only one who could get him to stop after one verse. Instead of scolding him or taking him away, he would just smile and sing harmony.

"You will be the best brother a guy could possibly have," Dr. Parini said.

Chris stopped singing but continued rocking. The back of his seat hit the wall with a rhythmic thump.

"No," he said. "Ben is."

13

Rosalie Sanchez could hear Dr. Parini in the next room. She had met the family when they'd checked in. Lovely parents, so tender with the younger brother, who seemed high-functioning but a handful.

As she cleared a candy wrapper from the floor, she smiled at the soldier. She half-expected him to smile back. He had that kind of face, intelligent and sly and full of life, like he was holding something back. Like this whole thing was a prank. She found him very handsome; he reminded her of someone she couldn't quite name.

After years of nursing you got used to things. In this hospital Rosalie had been vomited on at least a dozen times, seen a partial decapitation, witnessed a man stab his father in the waiting room, seen a thirty-seven-year-old woman who weighed fifty-three pounds. Those were all traumatic in their own ways, but the soldiers were always the hardest to take. If they died, the families were always so devastated. If they lived, the odds were against them ever leading a normal life.

"Harrison Ford, that's who you look like," she said softly, changing the dressing on his left arm. "Back in the early days, like the old *Star Wars* movie—right?"

Star.

"I bet a lot of people tell you that. Okay, your arm looks good, soldier."

Star. Arm.

"Now, time to turn over."

Starm. Tarm. Turn.

As she began cranking his bed, she heard thumping and humming in the next room. A moment ago she'd heard the soft murmur of Dr. Parini's voice, but she wasn't hearing it now. The doctor might need some help.

On the way out, she glanced at Ben's monitor. His heart rate was strong. His brain waves were active. Very active. The shape of his brain had changed by a few centimeters, warped slightly into a new configuration. "I've seen worse, honey," she said. "You have to be strong, you know. Your brother needs you. And your mom and pop. Be right back."

Oww.

Owww owwww owwww.

Ouuuuuut!

The thumping became louder as she opened the door.

14

September 17

Breathe.

Ariela tried to stop hyperventilating. The minivan was too small, too confined, too fast. The only person talking was Chris. No one was answering, but Chris wasn't requiring an answer. His chatter had become white noise, protection against having to make awkward conversation. If Ariela had had to say a word, she would have screamed.

Thoughts careened inside her. All she could see was Ben's face—his handsome, sad, misshapen face, now reflected in the windshield, the tree, the sky, the rooftops. Just a few years ago, a guy like Ben would have died. But they'd medevaced him out of an arid, sandy village with five other soldiers, cut his head open to ease swelling, attached IV drips to his arms, stabilized him with techniques only developed in the last five years. They'd slashed away his shirt and screamed instructions over him in midair while escaping rocket fire. They'd gurneyed him across a tarmac into an overcrowded hospital in hundred-degree heat, laid him out before haggard, caffeine-fueled specialists, packed him up tight for shipment to the U.S. And all the while he hadn't known a thing, just lying there with his mutilated handsome face, just another case, another young life saved by technology and passion, another line item on the ledger of modern miracles, a life unlost.

She had felt relief and comfort seeing his face, feeling his breath inches away. She had expected—what? Mutilation maybe, exposed bone or missing features, a horror movie image. He was blessedly intact and beautiful. Still, the sight scared her. It wasn't the scars or the bandages, but something in the shape, a cant of the right side, an angle different enough to make his face somehow horribly wrong, in the way that a small defect undermined the humanness of a sculpture, a painting, a wax likeness.

And now, here was his face again, dappled in the leaves, shape-shifted among the clouds, angled in the rooftops, smiling, laughing, singing, more real to her than he had been in person.

The guilt of it all squeezed her like a wet glove—the beauty of the imagined Ben, the revulsion of the real. It made her doubt her loyalty and her empathy.

"I'm writing a poem about Ben," Chris announced. "Ariela, writes poetry too, right?"

Ariela nodded absently. She had wanted to make the drive back to New York with the Brights and fly out of LaGuardia, not National. She had wanted to spend time with Mami and Papi, who she knew would make her feel better. But now she was having second thoughts.

"That's great, Chris, poetry is great," Mr. Bright replied, eyes intent on the traffic. "I—I spoke to the VA people after the briefing. They don't tell you everything unless you corner them. They don't know how long Ben will be in intensive care, but when he eventually gets home, we'll have to be ready. He had some leg damage and may not be able to walk. But it looks like we may be able to get grant money for a reconstruction of the house. They didn't say that was a done deal, though, and my sense is that we're going to face a lot of red tape."

"If anybody can do it, you can," Niko piped up from the back of the minivan.

"Maybe a sestina," Chris continued. "Or a villanelle. Actually those are easy. Pantoums are harder. Sestinas are the hardest, but they're more fun."

Mrs. Bright turned to her husband. Her face was wan and lined. She seemed brittle. "Will they pay for relocation while the house is being rebuilt?"

"I didn't ask," her husband replied. "Why would we need to relocate?"

"May I remind you," Mrs. Bright said, "that your other son has asthma?"

"Yes, I do," Chris said. "But it is much more occasional than it used to be. When I reached puberty, it became noticeably milder. The renewal for my albuterol prescription expires on November twelfth, and there is one refill after that, so we could order today and then again thirty days afterward without having to get a new prescription."

"You could stay at our house," Niko piped up.

"Thanks," Mr. Bright said. "But I think we can tough it out. Even do some of the work ourselves. Chris is a gamer—"

"Frank, please," Mrs. Bright said, her voice clipped and

raw. "Do it ourselves? With both of us working, and Chris in school, and visits to Washington?"

"We have to be positive—"

"Our lives have changed, Frank. We don't know how serious his injuries are, how long he'll need home care. Maybe years. Retrofitting the house isn't for hobbyists. We can't wait and wait on this."

Mr. Bright nodded. His knuckles were white on the steering wheel. "Okay, Lisa, that's a good point—"

"You can't just wish away what just happened and think everything's going to be okay!"

The van fell silent. Ariela felt the momentary urge to say something soothing, something observant and interesting about the surroundings, but she didn't. Words were worse than useless; they were the enemy, hooks on which to hang anger and misunderstanding.

He'll be fine. What if he won't?

We'll make a comfortable home for his rehab. What if it takes forever?

We'll just have to wait and see. As if we could do anything else?

Ben's life was all about management—recovery, rehabilitation, marking increments of progress. She felt for the Brights. They weren't wealthy. They would need help, expert help, and that would be expensive.

Ben would need to be surrounded by people who loved him.

Chris began snapping the elastic on the pouch behind the driver's seat. "What I like about the sestina is it's mathematical. You take the last word in each stanza and the next stanza preserves those same last words but in a different arrangement, retrograde pairs, which would be the pattern of 123456 going to 615243, and then 364125 and so on. Only they like to express it in letters, so that would be ABCDEF, then FAEBDC, then CFDABE, then—"

Ariela heard a brief, high-pitched sound that she took to be a stifled giggle, but immediately noticed that Mrs. Bright's face was deep red and she was choking on her tears in the passenger seat.

As Chris kept barreling on, Niko leaned forward and put his arm on Mrs. Bright's shoulder. She seemed to stiffen but she didn't brush him off, and he didn't let go.

"Fascinating, Chris," Mr. Bright said. "I think it's a perfect idea. If you want, you can start writing it now. And please, sweet guy, stop snapping the elastic."

"He can't write in the car, he gets carsick!" Mrs. Bright said sharply.

Chris dropped his hands and turned to stare out the window. "I will not get carsick," he said under his breath, closing his eyes. "I will not get carsick."

"I think we all have agreed that it isn't a good idea to plant the image," Mr. Bright said.

"Oh, I planted the image," Mrs. Bright replied. "The whole thing is psychological. Your driving has nothing to do with it."

"I will not get carsick. I will not get carsick!" Chris was rocking now.

"Easy, guy, I think I have a plastic bag," Niko said, unzipping his backpack.

"We have some in the glove compartment," Mrs. Bright said. But as she reached for it, her fingers missed the latch and her body lurched to the left. Behind them, a truck blew its horn. Mr. Bright was now veering into an exit ramp toward a large roadside rest stop.

Ariela closed her eyes and prayed.

"Did he puke?" Ariela asked Niko as he walked out of the rest stop men's room and toward the food court.

Niko shrugged. "I don't think so."

"Aren't you supposed to stay with him?" Ariela asked.

"He's fine," Niko replied. "He's in one of the stalls, composing poetry. He's like, 'I am in the bathroom now. Six words. Last word is *now* . . . ' I stayed in there for a long time. People would come in, I would just smile. One guy heard Chris, looked at me, turned white, and booked. Another guy, with this thick Long Island accent, says to me, 'He's autistic, huh?' I thought that was pretty rude, but I think he was really saying 'artistic.' I couldn't tell."

Ariela looked nervously over his shoulder. "The Brights told you not to let him out of your sight, didn't they?"

"You can hang in a men's room just so long before people start looking at you funny," Niko replied. "You pretend to be peeing but the sound component is missing. Guys get weirded out by that. Look, he's a big boy and he has the right to privacy. And I need some coffee, so would you please, please, please get me some if I stay right here and guard the door?"

Ariela glowered at him and turned toward the nearby Starbucks. Watching her go, Niko slumped against the tile wall. He felt about eighty-nine years old. Every muscle ached, and his head was pounding.

In the days since he'd heard the news about Ben, he'd barely slept. Each time he drifted off, he would see some version of the same scenario. Ben would be riding in a tank through an Iraqi village, his face wary and hard, scanning the hostile surroundings. The other soldiers, depending on the version of the dream, would be asleep, laughing, texting, looking at the GPS, downloading tunes, anything but paying attention. He, Niko, would be in the dream too, but he'd be lying on the path somewhere behind the tank. From his vantage point he could see a bomb in the road, off to one side, right in Ben's blind spot. It was one of those huge spidery devices like the one in *The Hurt Locker*, wired for maximum damage, and a grinning Al Qaeda guy stood hidden behind some rubble, hands poised over a detonator. Warning Ben was the only way to save his life, but for some reason, Niko would be crawling in the sand with only the use of his hands—and although he'd tried to scream, no sound would came out of his mouth . . .

At that point, Niko would bolt awake. For the rest of the night into morning, he'd be unable to go back to sleep because of the voices shouting in his brain: *You should have convinced Ben to stay . . .* or *You could have enlisted, so you could cover his back . . .*

But convincing Ben to do anything was like trying to talk the words off a street sign, and Niko would be more competent herding yaks for a living than serving in the Army. Ben had the backbone of a soldier. It was one of his many qualities—entertainer, scholar, lover, passionate believer.

None of which did him much good in a coma.

"Did Chris come out yet?" Ariela's voice called.

She was heading toward him with a steaming cup. Niko shook himself out of the reverie and looked over his shoulder at the bathroom door. "Not yet. Thanks for the joe."

"Ben's parents are eating at the Arby's," she said. "His mom's crying and his dad looks like he wants to leave her there."

"Guess Chris's time is up." Niko blew on his coffee, took a sip, and headed toward the men's room. "Once more unto the breach."

Niko pushed open the entrance door. The triangular rubber stop that kept it ajar earlier had been pushed aside, and he jammed it in place again. He walked a narrow green-tiled hall that led into the bathroom to the left. Once inside, the first thing Niko noticed was the relative quiet, the conspicuous absence of a voice track. By the sink, a dad was drying his little son's hands, and they quickly left.

"Chris?" Niko's voice echoed off the tiles. Chances were Chris had fallen asleep on the john. Only one stall door was still shut, Niko knocked gently. "Yo, dude, are you awake?"

At the force of his knocking, the door swung open slowly. No one was inside.

Niko quickly peeked in all the stalls, slamming the doors fully open against the metal walls to make sure Chris wasn't hiding. No dice. He stepped to the back of the bathroom and tried the window. It was bolted shut.

"Chris?"

He was gone. Disappeared without a trace. Niko cursed himself. Ariela had been right; he never should have let Chris out of his sight. He must have slipped away in a crowd, maybe even hiding himself on purpose.

Niko ran out the door. Chris had been wearing a New York Jets jacket. As he rushed toward the food court, Ariela ran up beside him. "Niko, what happened?"

"He ran out," Niko replied.

"What do you mean, '*ran out*'? You were right there!"

"I guess I didn't see him!"

"That's impossible. He'd have walked right by you!"

"I don't know, Ariela, he just did. I'll check the parking lot."

He raced out the glass doors. Chris was a wanderer. When he was feeling off his game, he liked to walk and walk. He couldn't have gone far, though. It had only been a couple of minutes. The sun was setting just beyond the cars, forcing him to squint.

There. A flash of characteristic Jets green and white disappeared behind a Jeep Cherokee.

Great. He'd managed to be taken by a total psycho stranger.

"Chris!" Niko shouted.

The Jeep started up. Niko darted out into the lot. To his left, tires screeched. Instinctively he jumped to his right, hooking his ankle on a trash can. He fell hard, the sun now blocked by a hulking shadow inches away.

He opened his eyes into the pebble-choked tire treads of a black Cadillac Escalade.

Someone in the car was screaming. Someone else was coming out the driver door. "Sorry!" Niko yelled, jumping to his feet.

He ran, his ankle throbbing. A half-dozen cars ahead, the Jeep was pulling out of the slot. It was rusted and run-down, its engine loud like a motorcycle. The green-and-white jacket was in the back. "Wait!" he cried out.

The Jeep stopped, and Niko nearly smacked into it.

The person in the back quickly turned. He looked about thirty years old and had red hair and freckles. From the passenger-side window, a wary-looking older woman asked, "Can I help you?"

Wrong person. Wrong assumption. Wrong everything.

"Sorry, looking for someone else," Niko said, quickly turning away. "Sorry."

Where was he? Niko scanned the lot. People were staring at him now. Niko cupped his hands and shouted: "I'm looking for a fifteen-year-old runaway in a Jets jacket!"

Niko raced back inside, past a uniformed security guard who was looking at him suspiciously. Inside, another couple of guards were headed into the men's room through the open door. Ariela emerged from the crowd, running toward him. "I can't believe you let him get away," she said. "Come with me."

Mr. and Mrs. Bright were near the restrooms, in agitated conversation with another guard. He asked Niko a few quick questions, mostly the same material he'd gone over with Ariela.

"He has autism," Mrs. Bright said. "He's very smart but he makes his own rules. It's not Niko's fault. Chris likes to walk.

When he doesn't want you to see him, he devises methods no one else would think of."

"Has the child run away before?" the guard asked.

"He's not a child!" Ariela said. "Are you sure he's not still in there—hiding in . . . I don't know, a duct or something?"

Before anyone could react, Ariela was heading toward the men's room. Niko followed her in and glanced around. The ducts near the ceiling were easily reachable, but they were thickly painted and obviously untouched for years. *If I were Chris leaving the men's room*, he thought, *where would I hide?* He turned his back to the stalls and walked slowly out of the bathroom, following the green-tiled wall into the short hallway. The jammed-open door did not have enough space behind it to conceal anyone. But it had been closed when he'd first gone back in to look for Chris. What *was* behind it?

Kicking the stop aside, Niko let the door close, revealing a shut broom closet.

Niko grabbed the doorknob, expecting it to be locked, but it turned easily. Yanking the door open, he peered into the shallow darkness.

Chris was sitting in a rectangular sink, his calves dangling over the front. Despite how extremely uncomfortable this appeared, he was fast asleep. A spiral notebook lay open on the floor next to him.

"Hey, buddy, time to wake up," Niko said, feeling a relief so sudden and giddy he thought he might pass out.

Chris could be prickly about wake-ups. But his eyes fluttered open like a little kid's. "So many miles we have come," he said. "Six words. Last word is '*come.*' I think that will be the fourth line. D. Which means I have to use '*come*' at the end of the fifth line in the next stanza. E."

Niko wanted to throw his arms around Chris, but that was a no-no, so he just helped him to his feet. Once upright, Chris immediately let go and picked up his notebook. "I think I may try something different. My teacher showed us a variation. You vary the number of words in the lines of each stanza. Six words in each line of the first stanza, five words in each of the lines of the second—"

"Hold that thought," Niko said, then called over his shoulder. "I found him—I found Chris!"

Chris laughed sharply. "I wasn't lost. I found this little room because I didn't like the toilet. It's very good for writing and thinking. But my butt hurts."

In a moment, Ariela and the Brights were all over Chris, crying and gushing and scolding, as Chris described his writing journey. The security guards smiled uncertainly, confused but relieved. A small crowd had gathered, wondering about the commotion.

"Please, let's take him right to the car," Mrs. Bright said. "He won't like this."

Taking Chris's arm, Niko nodded amiably to the crowd and rushed Chris toward the front door. "You're a star, dude," he said.

As they all stumbled gratefully into the parking lot, Chris fell silent. Niko gave Ariela a glance, and the expression on her face was immediately recognizable.

Ben, it said, would have loved this.

September 19

"Ben, this is Dr. Parini. Can you look at me?"

Look. Look. Look.

"Eyes flickering, uneven dilation of pupils, response to sound."

Sound. Sleep.

"Very good, Ben! That's great. I'm going to ask you yes-or-no questions. Can you blink one time for yes, two times for no?"

Yes.

"Is your name Ben Bright?"

Benbright.

"Is your name George Washington?"

Bengeorgeben.

"Can you see me, Ben?"

Seeben.

"Patient once again opening mouth, making clicking sounds and indefinite vowel aspirations. Ben? Will you please follow this light with your eyes?"

Brightbrightbright.

"Patient's eyes follow light stimulus. I'd say we were making some progress! Very good, young man. Big difference from yesterday, right, Nurse Sanchez?"

"Excellent progress! You are da man, Ben!"

Manben.

September 19

"You're seven minutes late," Ariela said, rolling her suitcase down the front steps toward Niko's car. "If there's any traffic, I'm going to miss my flight."

Niko held the passenger door open with one hand and waved to the Cruzes, who were standing on the porch. "It's all part of a diabolical plot to keep you here forever."

Ariela stuck out her tongue at him, although she was grateful for his upbeat attitude. The visit home had helped. She was glad she'd made the drive up from Washington, and she hated the idea that she was going back to college. It felt disloyal and indulgent, like she was shirking her real life for some kind of Brigadoon fantasy. Yet whenever she tried to define what her real life was—and she'd done little more than that since she'd been home—she came up blank. Her home, her friendships, her family, everything seemed a succession of temporary landing places, each unfamiliar in its own way. The intense exhilaration of college wasn't going to last, the security of home and high school had run its course, the future was a black hole. The grand design of life till now was simply this: everything you experienced and trusted was designed to push you away.

The worst thing was, she thought she'd already understood this. She thought she'd planned for it, at least psychologically.

She'd always known that her plan had included Ben. What she hadn't realized was how little of the plan didn't.

Niko had the radio on to the highly annoying WINS, where a radio announcer was yammering a traffic report in a staccato rhythm no human ever used except in traffic reports: "On-the-jam-cam-we're-seeing-a-stalled-tractor-trailer-in-the-left-lane-of-the-on-ramp-to-the-GWB-inbound-upper-deck,-at-least-forty-five-minutes-on-the-upper,-thirty-on-the-lower,-only-minor-delays-at-the-Lincoln-and-Holland,-East-Side-crossings-look-clear-but-watch-for-rubbernecking-delays-on-the-LIE-from-an-overturned-vehicle-at-Exit-twenty-four . . . "

"We'll take the Grand Central," Niko said, snapping the radio off.

"This feels so weird," Ariela said.

"Being late in a car with me? You should be used to it," Niko said.

"No, leaving so soon after seeing Ben," Ariela replied. "Leaving at all."

Niko was silent for a few moments. He turned onto the Meadowbrook Parkway, and a string of strip malls gave way to swaths of tired-looking greenery. "Do you believe in souls?" he asked.

"Yes, otherwise my feet would get dirty," Ariela said.

"When I saw Ben lying there, I thought about my Uncle Petros."

"Your Uncle Petros who died? Wait. He looked like Ben when he was young?"

"No, the way he looked in the casket. At the funeral."

Ariela felt her stomach turn. "Niko, that thought will disgust me for the rest of the year."

"I don't mean he *looked* like him—"

"Your uncle was fat and bald, and the hair sticking out of his nose looked like a small water vole trying to escape. No offense."

"He loved you too, Ariela. Actually, he was a really great guy, and when I knew I was going to the funeral and had to actually see him dead, I was expecting to faint. But I had the opposite reaction. As I stood over him, I immediately calmed down. All the pain he'd been experiencing? It was gone from his face. He'd been suffering for two years. Even though he looked made-up and artificial—the embalming and everything—in a funny way I was seeing *him* again. I was reminded of all the smiles and jokes and adventures and good times we had whenever he visited. I could hear his voice, and he was saying, '*Yia sou*, Nikolaos, I'm free now! I'm back again!' That's when I realized what a soul was. I know, it sounds ridiculous, I can stop now."

"No, go on. Shoot your other foot."

"I saw for the first time that people aren't their bodies. Even you and me—we're not just brains sending signals to eyes and vocal cords and . . . touch sensors or whatever. We're something bigger than that. We're communicating on a higher level."

"But Ben isn't dead, Niko!" Ariela said.

"I know. It's not a perfect comparison. I guess what I'm saying is, Ben's with us. No matter what happens, he's with us.

And compared to Uncle Petros, we're a thousand times luckier. Because eventually Ben's body will recover, and we'll have all of him again, in the flesh. Does that make sense?"

"By any chance, were you abducted by aliens?"

Niko slapped the steering wheel. "You never take me seriously."

"Just kidding. But you are very strange." Ariela sank back in her seat and felt her eyes closing from fatigue. She didn't want to rag on him too much. He meant well. "Mostly in a good way."

She fell into a deep sleep and was dreaming about the breakfast burrito at the Center Ground Coffee Shop when she heard a scream. "He *what*?"

Ariela's eyes blinked open.

It was Niko, his voice about an octave too high, talking on his cell phone while navigating Grand Central Parkway. "That's dangerous," she remarked. "You could get a ticket."

"I'm not *texting*. Okay, okay . . . Mrs. Bright? Wait. I'm putting Ariela on. Tell her." Niko's face was beaming as he handed Ariela the phone.

"Um, hi, Mrs. Bright," Ariela said. "He's driving, so—"

"Ariela? You won't believe this." Mrs. Bright let out an uncharacteristically raucous laugh. "Ben talked."

Ariela nearly dropped the phone. In trying to come up with a response, she emitted something between a word and a squeak.

"Not *talk* talked," Mrs. Bright went on. "He didn't perform Hamlet's soliloquy. But he did make sounds."

"Like, word sounds?" Ariela asked.

"Well, not really. But responses," Mrs. Bright replied. "Last night they asked him something and his eyes moved. This morning they did the same thing, and he opened his mouth and vocalized. Apparently this is great progress."

"It's *incredible* progress—woo-hoo!" Ariela said. She lurched across the seat and gave Niko a hug. He swerved into the next lane, forcing a yellow cab to jerk to the left and honk loudly.

"Thank you, good morning!" Niko called out.

"They say it's still too early to tell," Mrs. Bright went on. "The length of his coma may indicate serious brain trauma, but it's all very murky and they have seen similar cases with remarkable recoveries. Palo Alto is looking more and more likely. That's where the best treatment center is. But we'll take that when it comes. I just thought you and Niko needed to know."

Ariela could barely sit still. Her feet were dancing of their own accord. "I wish there were something I could do."

"Oh, Ariela, you were here for his return, and he knew it, sweetheart. Who's to say your presence wasn't the reason for his progress?"

Ariela tried to reply, but her throat closed up. "Thanks. Love you," was all she managed.

She gave the phone back to Niko, who said a quick good-bye as he pulled into the LaGuardia Airport entrance. Ariela fought back tears. She envisioned Ben in that bed right now, looking up at Dr. Parini, wondering who she was, wanting to talk, unable to utter a real word. Did he know where he was? Did he know how he got there? What did he remember? What was he trying to say? Was he afraid? That last question hung in the air as the American Airlines sign loomed, and the idea that she was leaving home nearly made her sick. "I—I can't do this."

"You have to," Niko said gently, putting a hand on her shoulder. "He's strong. He's the strongest person I know. He's going to get through this."

"I know. It's just that—" She paused. She knew Niko would trivialize the thing she was about to say. A sharp noise made her jump, and she turned to see an airline traffic guard rapping on the window. "It's too embarrassing. And I have to go."

Niko popped the trunk and they both quickly got out. "No need to be embarrassed in front of me," he said as he reached in for her luggage. "I've seen you naked."

"You have not!"

"At the beach that time you took off your bathing suit in public."

"I was four!"

"I was three. You think I'd forget that? Tell me what you were thinking, or I'll construct something in my fertile imagination and use it as my status update."

He let Ariela's luggage down and she pulled up its telescoping handle. For a moment she thought about giving him a quick good-bye and booking. But she knew Niko would be the only person she could talk to face-to-face about this for a long time. "Okay. Here's what I can't stop thinking about. I want to be here when he says his first word. I want that word to be 'Ariela.' I want to see him take his first steps."

"You sound like the mother of a newborn."

"I should slap you. You wanted to know, and that's how I feel."

Niko reached around behind her neck, drew her gently toward him, and gave her a kiss on the forehead. "Keep looking forward. Live your own life. That's the best thing you can do for yourself, and for him."

"You're so profound all of a sudden. Did you just think of that?"

"I'm reading a *Star Wars* novel. I think it was Yoda. I fixed the syntax."

She gave him a big hug and stayed there until the guard banged on the hood of Niko's car.

November 11

MEMORY BOOK

Ben Bright

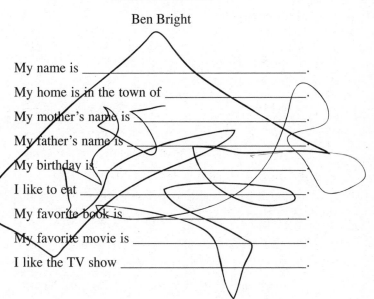

My name is _____.

My home is in the town of _____.

My mother's name is _____.

My father's name is _____.

My birthday is _____.

I like to eat _____.

My favorite book is _____.

My favorite movie is _____.

I like the TV show _____.

December 2

Report on Poetry Project 12

Mr. Hobbes

Nicholson School

Chris Bright

Today I wrote more of my sestina and most of it was
not good in fact terrible becasue it is hard to make
each stansa have a different number of of words which
is not standard but my own variation and also I forgot
some the end words and had to do ssttza 3 over again
and I got mad. I got so mad I went into my brothers
room his name is BEN of course he wasnt there but I
sat on his bed and I remembrd the last time I got mad
at homework and he helpd me but it wasn't in writing
it was in math and he tought me to use excel and I
thought well a sestina is mathemtaical so I can use
ecxel so I wont make mistakes keeping the end words
in the right place. Its really pretty easy all you need
to do is write ONLY ONE stanza but you write one

line in each row so you have six rows which are your
template and you make a column to the left where you
put A in the first row and B in the second row and C in
the third row and D in the fourth row and E in the fifth
rown and F in the sixth row like this

A

B

C

D

E

F

and then like I said next to each letter in the second
column is where you write the six lines of the second
stanza but just one line in each row so there will be
one line next to each letter. Then you take the last
word of the line and you copy it into a column on the
right so it will look all together like this

A   first line of stanza ending in word "end1"   end1

B   second line of stanza ending in word "end2" end2

C	third line of stanza ending in word "end3"	end3
D	fourth line of stanza ending in word "end4"	end4
E	fifth line of stanza ending in word "end5"	end5
F	sixth line of stanza ending in word "end6"	end6

but end1 etc are actual words. and then you skip a row and make six more rows just like the above bt the first column contains the letters F, A, E, B, D, C, but leave the second and third columns blank for now then you skip a row and then the next six rows in the frst column only contain C, F, D, A, B, E, skip a row and then the first column in the next six rows contain E, C, B, F, A, D, skip a row and then the next six rows contain D, E, A, C, F, B, skip row and then the next six rows contain B, D, F, E, C, A because that is the form of the sestina that we learned. You leave the middle column blank because that's where you write your stanza and i started to use a long embedded IF function but then i learned about the VLOOKUP function and i realized I could use it in the right column to get the end word right, so I used =VLOOKUP($A$10,$A$3:$E$8,5) in the third column of the first row of the second stanza but the numbers would be different if youre columns were in a different place so the referenses would change in case you want to try it. anyway the first element changes as you enter the formula with each row, so the third column of the secnd row of the second stanza would be =VLOOKUP($A$11,$A$3:$E$8,5) and right under it would be =VLOOKUP($A$12,$A$3:$E$8,5), and you keep doing that till the sixth row and then you skip a row and start the whole thing again for the next four stanzas making sure to adjust the first variable apropriatly, and then for the envoy its pretty easy just pick up from the first stanza E4, E7, next row E6, E5, next row E8, E3. And then you wont make any mistakes when you write your sestina.

An anagram of sestina is I assent. Also It's sane. And Eats sin.

© by Christopher Ian Bright.

20

December 14

It happened in the bookstore, and then again at Prince Hall.

The first incident was the piping of "In the Bleak Midwinter" over the speakers on November 29, while she was shopping for a biography of King Henry VIII. Christmas songs, she realized, were designed to lay dormant for months and then jolt you with joyous sense memories of cocoa-quaffing and gift-wrapping that led to an irresistible urge to shop. But for her the jolt was a shock of despair. "Bleak Midwinter" was Ben's favorite holiday tune and the title of a war movie he loved. She'd last heard it at Roosevelt Field Mall almost a year earlier, where Ben had impulsively spun her away from the sweater rack and kissed her.

The second had occurred during lunch moments ago. Until today Prince had been her favorite refuge, a Hogwartsian womb of vaulted ceilings and dark-wood wainscoting. It also had perfect acoustics for a spontaneous outbreak of the Handel "Hallelujah Chorus," which under ordinary circumstances would have had her on her feet screaming away with the sopranos, but today made her nearly hyperventilate. Mostly because she and Ben had once joined in on just such an outbreak in Grand Central Terminal with a group of Eastport chorus kids.

She had been doing so well till now. The reports about Ben

had been arriving regularly from Atherton, California, where Mr. and Mrs. Bright had been living with friends. His progress had been steady and promising. He was responsive to stimuli and "vocalizing," which brought to mind singing scales but actually meant making sounds and sometimes actual words.

These reports always filled her with hope and excitement. College was such a disconnect from her old life. It was about present and future, creating a life from scratch, a timeline with the starting point of Arrival.

Christmas changed everything.

Christmas was about everything good in the past that made you realize how much your life sucked now. Which was why she'd hiked all the way off campus in the snow to the environmental center, where she could get lost for a few hours in the forest and not have to brood in front of everybody.

Her fingertips were growing numb, and she blew on them as she walked among the trees. Her attempt to escape her own Ghost of Christmas Past was failing dismally. Ben, intact and full of life in all his imagined wonderfulness, had followed her here.

She became suddenly aware of footsteps crunching through the thin veneer of snow. She stopped cold.

The footsteps stopped too. Instinctively she turned but saw no one. "Hello?" she called out, her voice brittle in the thin air.

A deer, maybe. Although deer were quiet. And big enough to see.

She'd wandered pretty deep into the woods. Not too deep, she hoped. She turned to go, facing downhill toward the entrance, and realized that the pine trees were aligned in a matrix of perfect rows and columns. Probably some clumsy six-ties environmental-engineering project. But it meant she had a clear shot out.

The footsteps had stopped completely. She began walking, slowly at first, then briskly.

One of the trees had a visitor. A hooded figure in black.

She gasped and jumped back. He stepped backward too, his eyes wide from within the penumbra of a black hood.

Scrambling for her shoulderbag, she blurted out, "I have mace!"

"Whoa, easy," came the reply.

"Don't come near me." Immediately she remembered her mom's oft-told story of how she'd once scared away a mugger in New York City. And so she took the cue and began singing at the top of her lungs: "*Oh, say can you see, by the dawn's early light . . .*"

A smile flickered beneath the eyes. "*What so proudly we hailed by the twilight's last gleaming . . .*" he joined in, in a tenor descant that harmonized perfectly.

He was smiling. He looked normal and vaguely familiar.

Oh, great. Suddenly, with her little canister clasped tightly in her hand, she felt ridiculous. As the song died on her lips, the guy shrugged. "Sorry, didn't mean to scare you. You have a great voice."

"Who are you?" Ariela asked. "Do you make a habit of following girls into the woods?"

"What makes you think I didn't think you were following me?" he said, then frowned. "Wait . . ."

Everything about him screamed Sensitive Midwestern College Guy. "You're a Chase student, right?"

He shook his head. "The Naz. Jared."

"You just said three words in English, so why do I feel I need a translator?"

"Sorry. I go to Mount Morris College of the Nazarene and my name is Jared. You?"

"Chase. And Ariela."

Jared shrugged. "I understood that perfectly. And I should have figured, from the way you talk."

"That my name was Ariela?"

"That you went to Chase. You sound smart. And like you're from the East."

"To people in California, this here is the East."

"Is that where you're from, California? Is that why you're shivering?"

"No. You were right about the East. New York. And I need to get inside someplace warm."

"I have a car."

"How convenient. Race you to the parking lot."

She took off at a sprint. Just beyond the ersatz forest, to the left, was a dangerously steep decline. She nearly fell but made it intact to the parking lot, where one ancient, rusted gray Corolla sat alone. "Is this yours?" Ariela asked.

Jared was huffing and puffing, the left side of his hoodie coated with dirt and brown grass. "Yes. Sorry."

Ariela couldn't help but laugh. "About the car, or your clumsiness?"

"Both," he said, brushing himself off. "Let me."

Ariela tried to pull the door open, but it was jammed shut. "You lock your car door—here? I thought only New Yorkers did that."

"Hang on." Jared turned his back to the car and gave the door a sharp kick. With a loud creak, the door opened. "It's not locked. Just old. Easier to open from the inside, I promise."

It took a few tries for Jared to start the car, and his forceful thrusts of the clutch sounded like the chomping of some metallic monster jaw. As they ascended Higgins Street, the engine's groan was so deep and pervasive that it was more felt than heard, even as it blotted out all other sound. "*If you want, I can let you off here so no one sees you!*" he shouted.

But Ariela couldn't make out the words clearly. "*What?*"

"*In case you're embarrassed!*" he said, swerving toward the curb.

"*No, keep going!*"

After a tenuous moment when it seemed they might roll back down the hill, Jared pulled into a diagonal parking space near Center Ground. The engine died with a tubercular wheeze.

"Hey, a smartcar. You didn't even have to turn it off," Ariela said.

"Yeah, but will I be able to turn it back on?" Jared asked, his hand hovering tentatively over the keys.

"Well, you can stay here and experiment," Ariela said, forcing open the passenger door, "or you can have a cup of coffee with me. My treat. For bringing me back alive."

He followed her into the shop, where they both ordered coffee and a plate of snacks to split, and settled into the padded seats by the window overlooking campus. "I saw a play here once," Jared said. "*The Threepenny Opera*. I mean, not *here* here. In the theater. My big sister was in it."

"Before my time. I'm a freshman," Ariela said.

As Jared sipped his coffee, steam encircled his face. His hood was down now, revealing an unruly, but not unpleasant, spillage of brown curls, a long and thoughtful face like an El Greco painting, eyes wide apart and deep brown. "It was great. But what do I know? I'm an engineering major."

"You have a good stage face," Ariela said. "Dark features, wide-set eyes."

"Whatever. Thanks." Jared's face turned bright red. "So you're a theater major?"

"Well, I like musicals. I did them in high school. But I'm not sure I want to—"

"Which roles?"

"Maria in *West Side*, stuff like that. Soprano."

Jared grinned. "Are you doing something here? I'll come see you."

"They're not doing a musical this fall. So maybe next year."

"Cool."

They blew on their coffees. Suzanne and a couple of Ariela's friends stopped by and chatted. She introduced Jared. He seemed to know one of them. They ate their snacks. He said good-bye, left, and was able to start the car. The time passed quickly and Ariela felt warmer.

"Hmm," Suzanne said, watching the Corolla clank off. "Pretty hot."

Their friend Cameron nodded. "So's the car."

"I'll invite him back so you can get intimate with them both," Ariela said.

Suzanne smiled as she got up to go. "No-o-o-o comment."

In moments, Ariela was the only one left. She had been feeling good for the first time since lunch, but now she began to shiver.

She wasn't sure if it was because of the cold, or the fact that during the time she'd spent with Jared she did not, and did not feel the compulsion to, mention Ben.

21

December 30

Enough. It hurt.

"Ben, that's fantastic!" Dr. Larsen said.

Dr. Larsen was old. And nice. He had yellow and gray hair.

Thank you.

"Can you read aloud what you wrote, Ben?" the doctor asked.

Yes. Ben.

"Don't rush it," Dr. Larsen replied, acting like he'd heard nothing. "It's okay. Take your time. Say what it is that you just wrote."

I said, Ben. Ben. I just wrote Ben. "Mm. Mahng K."

"Yes!" Dr. Larsen was applauding now, but softly. "You are Ben. Okay, can you tell me, is your name Ben Franklin?

Nod for yes, shake your head for no. Answer if you can."

No. I don't think so.

"Come on, Ben, nod for yes, shake for no."

Okay. There. No.

"I'm not seeing it or hearing it, Ben. But that's okay. Can you blink once for yes, twice for no."

Okay.

"Excellent! Now, once for yes, twice for no—is your name Ben Bright?"

Yes, that's what you told me. Here, a blink.

"I see the blink, good! Can you speak your full name?"

Ben Bright. Right?

"You're doing incredibly well, but I don't hear anything. You need to take your time and listen to your own voice as it comes out. Try to talk as you exhale, okay?"

Ben Bright. Ben Bright. Ben Bright. "Aaahnng. Eyyyk. Aaah."

Dr. Larsen was beaming. "Amazing! We are making such progress. Are you tired? Blink please."

No.

"You must be exhausted."

No. Not tired. No! "Nnnnk."

Dr. Larsen's eyebrows went way up. "What's that, Ben? Is that a yes?"

Why can't you listen to me? "Ohhh. M."

The doctor nodded, ignoring his question. "Fantastic. Okay, I'll be going now."

Why can't anybody tell me why I'm here?

"You know, your family will be visiting tomorrow. I

understand your fiancée will be here too. Isn't that great? You'll be surrounded by love."

Family?

"Let's see . . . " Dr. Larsen said, glancing down at a chart. "Ariela. And Mom and Dad and Chris. They will be so happy to see how far you've come!"

Don't know those people.

The doctor put his hand gently on Ben's arm. "Better get a good night's sleep, Ben."

Will you please answer my questions?

Why am I here?

When can I go?

Are those people really my family? Why don't I know them?

Who are they?

"Big day tomorrow, Mr. Bright!" Dr. Larsen said as he left the room. "See you then!"

Don't go.

Tell me what happened to me.

Tell me who I am.

Somebody, please tell me who I am!

22

December 31

"I'm sorry, that's bullshit, he doesn't look good. He looks terrible. He does. He's lost too much weight and his eyes don't focus and there's drool coming out of his mouth and every time he tries to speak the doctor acts as if he's just recited the Gettysburg Address."

Shut. Up. Just shut up.

The words were shooting out of Ariela like blood from a wound, but she couldn't stop. She could hear them echoing off the fake-wood partition of the diner booth, and people around them were averting eyes.

Sleep deprivation, that was the biggest part of it. She hadn't slept in days, and the red eye from Columbus to San Francisco had taken eight hours because of a delay at her layover in Phoenix. *Phoenix.* She couldn't imagine why on earth there would ever be a delay in a place like Phoenix, which had no bad weather.

Across the table, Mrs. Bright was looking at her with huge, kind, pitying, blue eyes. Ariela wanted to cry. "I can't believe I said that. Just shoot me, okay? Just take me outside and shoot me. I don't know what's wrong with me."

Mrs. Bright reached out and cupped Ariela's hands in hers. "I know. It's hard to see him after such a long time."

Ariela flinched but kept her hand still. She didn't feel like touching or being touched, but she stayed put out of politeness and gratitude for the fact that Mrs. Bright had picked her up at the airport and agreed to house her for a few days. And the act of touching, that gesture of forgiveness and inner strength, made Ariela feel about two inches tall. Ben was Mrs. Bright's son, her pride and joy, and Ariela had just ripped anything positive from their visit. "I'm so, so, so sorry," she said. "I'm just feeling tense and sad. And maybe a little angry at the doctors for acting like that. They don't know him. They have no right to talk to him like that. Like he's . . . an old person at a nursing home."

"They have to," Chris said. "Because his brain has been damaged in the cerebral cortex."

"Have one of these pickles," Niko blurted out, brandishing a gherkin and then popping it into his mouth. "They're good."

"They look like severed dragon tonsils," Ariela said.

Niko gagged.

"I'm having a grilled cheese, rye bread, no crust, white American cheese, grilled in extra-virgin olive oil," Chris said, looking up from a sheet of paper filled with doodles and cross outs, and words crammed into and over and around each other.

Mrs. Bright tapped Ariela's hand softly. "We're not only here for Ben, we're here for each other, so no need for an apology, ever." She smiled at her son. "We're all going through a lot."

"I'm writing my sestina," Chris said, "without my spreadsheet."

"He's using Excel to help with the meter," Niko explained.

"Not the *meter*. That doesn't make sense," Chris said. "The *construction*."

"Oh," Ariela said. She tapped her fork and noticed for the first time that Ben's father wasn't with them. "Is Mr. Bright joining us?"

"No," Mrs. Bright replied. "Not today."

"These tonsils sure are amazing!" Niko said brightly.

Ariela glanced away. Niko was talking with his mouth full, and the green goop nauseated her. Chris was in his Chris-world: Mrs. Bright was trying too hard to keep things cheery. The conversation was like dispatches from another solar system, and no matter how hard she tried, nothing out of her own mouth was constructive. She tried to breathe deeply, but the air was nasty, like they were too near the bathroom door or the chef was cooking iguana for lunch. Everything in Northern California smelled funny, even the outside air, which had a strange spicy odor like fermented herbs. This neighborhood, this weather—balmy and bright in the middle of winter—it should have lifted her mood, but it added to a feeling of disjointedness, as if she were on a movie set with a bunch of actors who had forgotten their lines. "Excuse me for a second, please," she said.

She headed toward the women's room, but the idea of another enclosed space made her feel ill. Instead she detoured to the front door and burst out onto the sidewalk.

Breathe.

She put her hand over her chest and felt her heart beating.

Across the street was a stretch of neat, trendy shops, with neat, trendy cars parked at perfect-looking curbside parking meters. It all seemed so pristine, like a slice of SoHo swept clean of people and dirt, buffed to a shine, and put under a sunlamp. It was oddly comforting, but it didn't stop her from wanting to sprint to the ocean and jump in while no one was looking.

Closing her eyes, she leaned against the wall and forced herself to take deep yoga breaths, to think about the visit, about Ben's attempts to talk, about his eyes as he saw her.

Did he know who she was? It wasn't clear. That was the most disturbing part.

"'Sup?" came Niko's voice to her right.

"Claustrophobia," she said, not bothering to open her eyes. "I'll be back in a minute."

"I'm feeling a little off my game too," he replied. "Mind if I join you?"

"Yes."

He stayed put, but honestly she didn't care. "Do you think he knew us?" he asked.

"Do you?"

"Oh, yeah!" Niko said. "Of course. Yes. I think." He paused. "Maybe not."

"What if doesn't remember us?"

Niko sighed. "He will. I think that kind of thing is hard-wired. It's got to be. But even if it isn't, he's still the same guy, right? Memory is like a sculpture that gets messed up. The rock is still there. You can just chip away and make another sculpture with what remains, and it'll be just as good. Even better."

"But the rock is smaller," Ariela said.

"Well, it's not a perfect metaphor," Niko replied. "Listen, there was something I needed to tell you. About what you brought up in there. Ben's parents. They haven't been together for a few weeks. You may have noticed her reaction to your question."

Ariela's eyes sprang open. "They're divorcing?"

"Just chilling for now. Things haven't been great between them. She's living in their friend's garage apartment and he's staying at a hotel in San Jose."

"Oh my god. But they're . . . "

"Perfect. I know. Guess things change." He shrugged. "Well, don't tell her I told you. She'll probably tell you soon enough. Just wanted you to know what she's going through, okay?"

He turned to go back inside, and Ariela followed, numb, thinking about a house full of humor and music and thoughtful conversation. About a place that always represented comfort and love. About four people she'd begun to think of as family.

About the world spinning aimlessly in space.

23

March 12

MEMORY BOOK

Ben Bright

My name is _____ Ben _____.

My home is in the town of _____ Esypor _____.

My mother's name is _____ Lisa _____.

My father's name is _____ Fre _____.

My birthday is _____ March 6 _____.

I like to eat _____ is crem _____.

My favorite book is _____.

My favorite movie is _____ Ankoran _____.

I like the TV show _____.

Anchorman was funny. He laughed a lot. So he filled in that line.
Dr. Larsen was going to come soon. He would be very happy
to see a new word.

Ben got out of bed and stood. He felt dizzy, so he grabbed
hold of his walker. He pushed it forward and began to walk.
The walker scraped against the floor and made a creaky noise.

"Ben, where are we going?" Nurse Harold came into the
room. He had very thick glasses that made his eyes always look

surprised. He was also going bald. He was always asking questions, too, even when the answer was obvious. Like now. He was going walking.

"Walking," Ben said.

"I'll help you," Nurse Harold said. "Where would you like to go?"

Only one place he could be going. He went there a lot. There wasn't much choice. It was bed, bathroom, bed, bathroom. But Harold always wanted him to talk. He was always trying to get Ben to do that.

Ben focused on Harold's face. His features were bubbling in and out. "To the. Home. I need unlock. White what ashnur."

Harold nodded. "You have to make pee pee. Very good, Ben. Let's go."

He let Harold help him. He needed Harold's help. He kept trying to walk to the bathroom by himself, but it was too hard. Soon he would be able to in the night when Harold wasn't working and then just leave it there. And when Harold came back he would tell him to look! And Harold would say, Did somebody help you? Then Harold would flush the toilet and say that the night people were so lazy. But Ben would tell him, I did it myself! But that was not happening today. Ben was weak. He hated feeling weak. Maybe Harold knew when he would be better. Ben turned to ask him. "I hate feeling. Better. When is bathroom."

Nurse Harold smiled. "Almost there."

Ben felt angry. Sometimes Harold understood, but sometimes he was just like the others. The people answered questions Ben didn't ask, they nodded and pretended to understand. They did things Ben told them not to do. They asked Ben to repeat himself. Ben would say the exact same thing, the exact same way—and they'd act like he said something different. Sometimes they'd get his meaning. Sometimes they'd laugh, like he told a joke. Sometimes they'd keep asking him until they got bored. All this, even though he never changed a word.

He reached the bathroom and stood over the toilet, fumbling with the folds of his robe.

"Uh-uh-uh, not yet, soldier." Nurse Harold began turning him around slowly. "You have to sit. Come on now, don't let go. Keep it in. Turn around and sit."

Ben did as he was told, and Harold kept talking. "The Mets swept a doubleheader today, three to one and twelve to ten. Not exactly a pitcher's duel, that last one."

Harold loved baseball. He kept Ben's TV tuned to it. The images all moved around so fast. Just when you focused on one guy, you'd see someone else. It made Ben feel dizzy. He had to close his eyes. He'd say turn it off, but most of the time no one listened.

Harold was starting to lift him back up, but Ben wasn't finished. So he said so: "I'm navigating."

"Excuse me?" Harold asked.

He couldn't understand *I'm not finished?* "At the back of the water."

"Okay, so let's get you to bed, then. Upsy daisy!"

Ben repeated himself once more, louder. Sometimes he

thought Harold was doing this on purpose. "I'm in the form of it!"

"What? I don't understand you, Ben!" Harold said.

I understand everything YOU say. "I crab it. Green. And go away!"

He wasn't letting go.

Ben pulled his arm away. Harold's hand sprang back and yanked out an IV needle from Ben's arm. Blood spattered on Harold's uniform and a bit of it got on Ben's face and into his mouth. It tasted funny, like something familiar, but he didn't know what.

Now he was finishing.

Harold was yelling at him. Harold was taking the bandage off Ben's arm and putting in a new needle. Dr. Larsen had entered and was now standing in the doorway, asking questions. His voice was soft. Harold's answers were loud.

Ben stopped listening because he had to concentrate. He heard Harold say, "Why didn't you tell me? Why did you have to make such a mess?"

Ben answered the truth. That he did tell him. And the whole point was not to make a mess. "Ardy."

In moments, he was feeling much better. Harold helped him finish up, then escorted him back to the bed, where Ben could give his memory book to the doctor.

And sleep.

24

May 23

"Sorry, the answer is no," Ariela said. "Finals are not going well. In fact, they are sucking."

Jared twirled a forkful of pasta and nodded. "That sucks."

"Thank you, that shines an interesting new light on what I just said." The band at the Village Inn was Wu Kitchen that night, and Suzanne was vocalist. The group was awesome, but Ariela was having trouble concentrating. She sipped her Blue Moon, noticed the slightly hurt and confused expression on Jared's face, and came to the realization she had just said something incredibly snotty. Mustering what she hoped was a reasonably impish smile, she kicked him under the table. "Hey . . . I'm joking."

"Sorry, I'm brain-dead after a week of statistics and linear algebra," Jared said.

"At least you're done," Ariela replied. "I'm still pissed at the econ final today. I only stayed up all night drilling on the theories, and it was all quant stuff. I hate macro. Anyway, two down, two to go."

"Anything I can help you with?"

Ariela nodded. "Yup. Tomorrow's Music History. Can you list all the influences on Gabriel Faurè? And what do you know about Carl Ditters von Dittersdorf?"

Jared laughed. "Is that a real guy?"

"Yes, but we're not studying him. I just like to say the name." Lucy the waitress was passing by so Ariela called out for two more Blue Moons.

"I'm okay," Jared said.

"No, you're not," Ariela replied. "We're going drink for drink. Equals. To avoid at all costs the scenario of wasted-college-girl-pathetically-leaving-herself-open-for-another-Take-Back-the-Night-story. In fact, my friend Elyse is on the school Beer-and-Sex Committee and is sitting at the next table so she will watch over us like the Angel Gabriel and be our witness—right, Elyse?"

No one at the next table replied, but that wasn't the point anyway. Ariela wasn't sure what the point was, except that the year was coming to a close and she was heading back to New York for a summer internship at a dance company, her grades having plunged into the toilet this semester, and sitting across from her at the moment was wonderful, sweet Jared Combs, whom she wouldn't see again until the fall. All year he'd been finding time to hang out with her on campus. He'd gone to a concert or two with her, cheered for her at a so-called Baby Drama class production that wasn't very good, been there to soothe her ruffled feathers at least a dozen times for two dozen reasons, been her chauffeur into Mount Morris a dozen more, and all the while somehow swinging a 3.8 at the Naz without any apparent effort.

She owed him.

"Seriously, what time is your music final?" Jared asked.

Sometimes, however, he could be a mother hen.

Ariela took a deep breath to gather patience. "Not till eleven, Mom, so I'm good. After the next song, I'm out of here."

The next song was new and fresh, and it brought them both to their feet. She watched Jared as she danced, the way he eyed her. They'd been playing this game all semester. He'd been amazingly cool, not pushy, not too sexual, seemingly okay with things the way they were. He gave her freedom and space, and she adored him for it.

The number ended with a segue into a ballad. She felt Jared pulling her away from the bar, toward the door, and she pulled back. She protested about the beer left undrunk and the unpaid tab, but he insisted he had taken care of everything. Within moments she felt the rush of a late spring breeze and the overwhelming quiet of night. The tables outside were full of couples in muffled conversation, but Jared rushed her out too fast for her to recognize faces.

They stumbled up Center Path, laughing at something, she wasn't sure what. Her stomach was beginning to hurt from the laughter but Jared wouldn't let her sit on the benches. By the time they arrived at the dorm, she was having a hard time staying upright. Jared walked her into the building and then her room, and in the semidarkness set her down on the bed.

She felt better prone. Her lights were out, so his face was softly lit from the streetlight outside.

Have you always looked this good?

She wasn't sure for a moment if she'd actually said those

words or thought them. "I thought them," she finally decided aloud.

Jared's smile made her ache. "Say what?" he asked.

"Okay," she said. "You may. I say you may."

He laughed. "Ah, it's Dr. Seuss night. What, I pray, do you say I may?"

"Ow, the meter is all wrong," Ariela said. "Chris would kill you."

"Chris who? Is that your boyfriend?"

It wasn't until that moment, after two semesters-ful of companionship with this guy, after he'd become friends with her friends and a fixture on campus, that she realized their cozy relationship had been propped up by fraud.

The lie had begun from the first time they'd met. She could have mentioned Ben but didn't, and somehow that choice had locked her in, forced her to construct a half-persona and call it whole.

He knew something was up. He wasn't stupid. She was wearing an engagement ring, for god's sake. But for all their time together, he knew so little about her. He had no idea what she was going back to, the working and waiting, the progress reports and plane trips, the anxiety and guilt. Still, he never, ever questioned or mistrusted her. Never made her feel like anything but beautiful and smart and witty and fun. He never pried. Until now.

"No. Chris is not my boyfriend." She reached up and cupped both hands behind his head, pulling him closer. "My boyfriend he is not."

She smelled the sweetness of the fabric of his shirt, the thickness of his breath. She let her mouth go slack and anticipated the weight of him, the comfort of his body in the lonely night.

"Ariela," he said, his voice landing with soft grace on each syllable.

She hummed a half-reply, but he took her hands in his and pushed them away. Her body rolled slightly with the mattress as he stood. "I have to go," he said. "I'm leaving the wastebasket by your bed if you need it, but I hope you don't."

What was he saying? "Wait," she said.

"I'll call you in the morning to make sure you're up for the final, okay?"

"But—but wait—"

"Hey, it's okay. Sleep well, Ariela. Good luck."

Before she could answer, he was gone.

The prick. Who did he think he was?

She inhaled deeply to yell at him, but at the top of the breath, the impulse left her.

25

May 25

FROM: Dr. Claes Larsen <clarsenmd@clinicpa.gov>
TO: Ms. J. Bright <jbright0523@eastportmail.com>
Subject: Fw: Progress Report, Benjamin Bright

Hello, Ms. Bright! Once again, Benjamin has shown remarkable resilience and an extraordinary capacity to learn. He is speaking more clearly, his thoughts attaching often to appropriate vocabulary, resulting in effective expression, which fluctuates in proportion to the amount of his physical rest, and also to fatigue of extended vocalizing. He makes himself understood about 50% of the time now, which, given the length of his stay, puts him easily in the top quintile of patients I have ever seen. We are working him hard, and he is a hard worker!

I know his memory remains your biggest concern, and in that regard I also have positive news. Ben remembers staff almost all the time now, and even correctly identified his nurse, Harold Yu, spontaneously by name (without prodding!) after Mr. Yu's absence of four days. We have begun tailoring his therapy to stimulate and strengthen long-term memory. He identifies photographs of family and repeats personal historical data we have trained him to remember. However, those memories appear to have a "shelf life" if not refreshed regularly. And attempts to prompt him to spontaneously recall teacher and family names, personal anecdotes, favorite entertainments, etc., have yielded somewhat tenuous results.

In summary, I would categorize his progress as excellent regarding large-motor skills, task completion, short-term concentration and memory, small-motor skills, temper control, and verbal communication. The lag in long-term memory is not unusual, but we would like to bring that category closer in line with the others.

I hope this message gives you as much hope and excitement about your son as we have. I anticipate we'll be able to release Ben within the year, and we will all miss him. He lifts our spirits and restores our faith in the work we do together. One extraordinary young man!

Best regards to your family,
Dr. Claes Larson

• • •

As Mrs. Bright read aloud the letter over dinner in her family kitchen, her voice grew thick and she brushed away a tear. Niko felt a little weepy, too.

From an iPhone resting on the table, Ariela's voice piped up scratchily. "I'm a mess. Someone is going to have to scrape me off the floor. I wish I could be there with you."

"We'll save you some champagne," Niko called out. "Actually, no we won't."

"I spoke to him on the phone," Mrs. Bright said. "He called me 'Mom.'"

"He said, 'I want to come home,'" Niko added.

Ariela was squealing. Chris had risen from the table and was examining the rail that had been built into the kitchen wall. While the Brights had been in California, he had boarded at his school, and they'd enrolled him in the summer session because he'd freaked out when getting on a plane to California and had to be taken off. So he hadn't seen Ben, and he hadn't seen much of the reconstructed house.

"Take this off," he said.

"It's for Ben, dude," Niko said. "He's going to need it to get around."

"Take this off!" Chris shouted. He stood there, staring at the rail, his face growing redder by the second.

"Ariela, I have to go," Mrs. Bright said, shutting the phone. She turned to face Chris squarely. "Chris, honey, please look at me."

"No! No no no no no! It's not right! Take this off!" He began pulling at the rail, then pounding it.

"Chris, stop it!" Mrs. Bright leapt from her chair. She threw her arms around her son and pulled him away from the wall.

Chris let out a strangled-sounding scream. He flailed his arms and stumbled, catching his foot on the table leg.

Niko ran toward them, trying to pry Chris away, but he and Mrs. Bright fell backward, into a granite counter. Her head hit with a dull thud and she dropped to the floor.

"For god's sake, Chris, what are you doing?" Niko grabbed Chris's sweatshirt and yanked it upward, inside out and over his head. Chris's arms shot up, temporarily immobilized, his vision blocked.

His shrieking was unearthly loud, even muffled by the fabric. Niko shoved him away from Mrs. Bright and spun him out of the kitchen. Chris thudded heavily on the living-room floor.

He wouldn't have much time. Chris was capable of violence if he got too riled up and wasn't taking his meds properly. Niko rushed to Ben's mother, who was slumped unconscious on the kitchen floor. "Hey . . . hey," he said, gently shaking her. "Are you okay?"

Her eyes fluttered open and she winced. "Yeah. Fine." She reached around to touch the back of her head. "That's going to be a big bruise."

Without waiting another moment, she rose from the floor and went into the living room.

Chris was lying on the carpet. His hands were still over his head, the underside of his sweatshirt rising over his fleshy, naked torso like a peeled banana. He was breathing steadily and hard now, muttering to himself.

Mrs. Bright sat at his side. "Christopher Ian Bright, pull your shirt down and talk to me."

Chris fell silent. He began mumbling again but didn't comply. Niko sensed the confinement was comforting to him.

Mrs. Bright exhaled and shook her head. "Thank you so much, Niko," she said softly.

Thank you? Niko was still shaking. Chris could have killed her. "If you want, I can live here to help out, until . . . "

"I'll be all right," Mrs. Bright said. "Ben's father is arriving tomorrow morning. We have lots to talk about."

He tried to pick up her meaning, but her eyes were distant and cryptic. "Are you two . . . ?"

She shrugged. "I don't know. Say a prayer, okay?"

"Will do," Niko replied.

Together they pulled down Chris's sweatshirt. He looked at them with a slightly preoccupied but tired expression, as if nothing had happened. "Mr. Hobbes gave me a B plus . . . ," he said, his words dissolving into a yawn.

Niko and Mrs. Bright each hooked one of Chris's arms over their shoulders and walked him slowly to bed.

26

August 3

MEMORY BOOK
Ben Bright
—page 5 —

I RemEmBR ThE zoo WERE
ThERE WER BIG FISH. I wAz A
little BoY.

I ATE ISKREam FroM A GUY IN
a TRUck.

YESTERDaY I TALKED To a MaN
ON THE FON aND HE Ws MY Da.
HE Is CMING ToDa.

I Saw a ShoW AbouT A TRAIN AN
I Was ON a TvaIN WHEN I Was
HOM.

Ben sat up straight. They were always telling him to sit up straight. He held a manila folder in his hand tightly. He had worked all day on his project down at the common room. The therapist had helped him.

Dr. Larsen was talking to a bunch of people. Suddenly he ran into the hallway and then ran back in. "My boy, are you ready?"

"Yes," Ben said. He had learned that if he did a few things Dr. Larsen recommended, people were more likely to understand him:

Plan out the exact words you're going to say. Think about them before speaking.

Say only a few words at a time.

Try to hear each word as it comes out of your mouth.

He had been doing this for a long time. But lately people seemed to be responding better.

Mr. Bright poked his head in, smiling. "Heyyyy, Benny! 'Sup, my son?"

Ben smiled. He had glasses now, and they slipped down the bridge of his nose, but at least faces were easier to see. He let the man hug him and then handed the man the manila folder. "For. You."

The man stared at him funny. "Wow! Okay! What's this all about?"

"Birth. Day," Ben said carefully.

The man opened the folder and looked at the card. It was a drawing of a baseball bat and a baseball. Also a car. Underneath it, Ben had drawn HAPPY BIRTHDAY, DAD! That was what they told him to do.

The man's face calmed down. Then it got dark and he started to cry. "That's beautiful. That's the most beautiful thing I ever saw. Thank you, Benny." He crouched down and put his arms around Ben. Ben could see Dr. Larsen standing behind the man, smiling. He pretended to hug the air and gestured at the man. He was telling Ben to hug the man.

Ben hugged the man who was his dad.

"You're. Welcome." He had almost forgotten to say it. Saying it was part of the plan.

"We're going to get you home soon, Ben," the man said. "The house is all set up for you. You're going to feel so good. Chris talks about you all the time. Niko goes over there to help your mom. He's been amazing to her. And Ariela's almost finished her internship, so she'll be free for a few days before she goes back to college. We're going to have a huge party. A hero's welcome."

Ben nodded.

The man frowned. "Did you get all that?" He turned to Dr. Larsen. "Did I . . . ?"

"You're fine," the doctor replied. "What do you think of that, Benjamin? You're going home soon. We have some excellent New York doctors lined up to help you."

"Home," Ben said. Home was a good place. He had seen pictures of it, and it looked nice. He wanted to be home. He wanted to have a father, too. Fathers and sons. Movies and TV shows had fathers and sons. He was happy he had a father. "You are. Father."

The man looked at Dr. Larsen, who quickly said, "Yes, this is your father, Ben."

Ben leaned forward. Sons knew their fathers. Sons loved their fathers. If you had a father, you loved him.

He had seen this man many times. He had seen the woman many times too. But he never saw them together, except in pictures. The doctors were going to let the two people take him out of the hospital, because they were his family. He thought he could remember his family sometimes. Sometimes he recognized a thing or two in the pictures. But they could have been anyone's pictures. Even though Ben was in many of them, he couldn't recall being there. He didn't know this man.

If he didn't know the man, then he couldn't be Ben's father.

"No," Ben said.

The man blinked, then blinked again. "No?" he said.

"No." Ben turned away. Maybe tomorrow his father would come.

"Ben, I have pictures. Pictures of you and me together." The man was digging in his jacket pocket.

Ben turned back. The man was holding out photographs. The top one was the man and a little boy. "That's me and you," he said.

He flipped to another photo, and another. The boy got bigger. The last photo was the man and Ben. Their arms were around each other, and they were outside. He showed another photo. Also Ben and the man. Then he took out his phone and showed more pictures.

Ben's head was hurting. He was tired of looking at pictures. The ones from the phone were shiny and hurt his eyes. Why didn't he know this man? Why did this man scare him? Why did all these people scare him?

"No," he repeated.

"Yes, Ben, yes," the man said. "You'll come home. It'll all feel familiar. You'll see. Just trust us, okay?"

Ben nodded.

Trust. Dr. Larsen talked about trust. Ben trusted Dr. Larsen.

Why wasn't Dr. Larsen his father?

27

August 8

NikoP: sup?

ACruz: im tired. i was up till 3 troubleshooting the website.

NikoP: sux

ACruz: im scared 2.

NikoP: here we go again. school? afraid ur only gonna get b pluses this yr? hahaha

ACruz: with my courseload, if they give lower than an f, thats what im getting. g minus.

ACruz: & thats not whats scaring me u dbag. y do u think im scared or r u just being provocative for once?

NikoP: yeah i know. actually now im feeling weird that i have to go away to school right after he gts back

ACruz: 1 thing at a time

NikoP: fo shizz

ACruz: i miss him

NikoP: me too. cant wait. 2 more days.

ACruz: i mean i miss HIM.

ACruz: the way he was, i mean. the way he used to be.

NikoP: well hes still him

ACruz: that sounds bad, oh god i didnt mean it that way, please shoot me now. you know. just sayin

NikoP: i know. no ones gonna shoot you. i know what u mean & i think about that too.

ACruz: thx

NikoP: meant to ask, u ever hear from that guy?

ACruz: what guy

NikoP: the one i met when i visited. the cornhusker who was drooling all over u

ACruz: jared is a sweet considerate guy unlike u. i told him about ben & he was totally cool. he said he had a sense all along. thats how sweet he is.

NikoP: b/c hes still hoping to get in yr pants

ACruz: have i told u lately ur an asshole?

NikoP: i love you too.

28

August 10

Ben felt nothing as he was wheeled through the door. He was expecting to feel something. He had seen a movie where a guy had come home from war all injured and not knowing who he was, and then when he walked in the door he started crying and he knew who everyone was.

He recognized the man and the woman who were his mother and father. He had seen them so many times at the hospital. Also the guy who was his friend, Niko. The girl, Ariela. He was going to marry her, which was a good thing. She was pretty, but every time she saw him she cried. He liked girls who didn't cry so much. There was a girl in the movie, she had dark hair and a beautiful sad mouth and he liked her. He wondered if he would meet her. The movie was in New York. He was in New York now, too, but this place didn't look the same. There were no yellow taxis. That movie had a lot of taxis.

Everyone was talking to him at the same time. There was a rug on the floor with a lot of patterns. He wanted to look at it, but people kept asking him to look up. They were standing next to him and taking pictures with their cameras. It was hard to hear the words with everybody talking, but a few times he heard Smile, and so he did. The problem was, smiling seemed to make people laugh very loud, so after three times he stopped doing it.

He heard Remember me, it's Wendy . . . it's Jeannie . . . welcome back . . . you look great . . . all kinds of things like those over and over. So many people expected him to remember them. Maybe this was some kind of exercise. Dr. Larsen was always asking Do you remember this, do you remember that? He thought being home would mean less remembering because it would be full of things remembered. But it wasn't. It felt cold.

He saw a couple of little children running in and out. They were cute, but they only wanted to look at him for a second and then run away. They were quiet, too, and quiet would be great right now. So it was too bad they didn't stay.

He looked down and saw a piece of chocolate cake on a plate in his lap. The girl was digging in with a fork and holding it to his mouth. Ariela. He lifted his right hand and took the fork from her. He didn't like the idea of someone else feeding him. Sometimes people tricked you. Sometimes they gave you bad drugs. He saw that on TV a lot. So he took the fork and fed himself and people began to applaud. He took another piece and they applauded again. The sound hurt his ears so he stopped eating. The woman who was his mom wiped his mouth with a napkin.

"Is this?" he said to her. "My. House?"

"I'm sorry?" she replied, kneeling and leaning her ear toward his mouth. "Say it again?"

"My house?" he asked.

"Yes," she said. "This is your home. This is where you grew up. I'm here, and Daddy is here, and your brother, Chris, and Ariela and Niko and all your friends and family."

"Oh." Ben looked around again. So many smiles, so much friendliness. And loudness. He saw a big sign hanging over a piano. He knew the words. They were all words he knew. It said WELCOME HOME BEN! He saw balloons that said WE LOVE BEN! Everywhere he looked, he saw Ben, Ben, Ben. But none of the people were from the hospital. Dr. Larsen wasn't there. These weren't his friends. He didn't know them. Dr. Larsen said this would happen. He said it might feel bad. It did. Why were they all so happy?

"Tired," Ben said. "I am. Tired."

"Okay, sweetie, this is pretty overwhelming, isn't it?" the woman said. She went around behind him and began pushing his wheelchair further into the house. "He's tired," she explained. "I'm going to get him to his new bedroom."

In the back of the kitchen, the man opened the door. The woman who was his mother placed the wheelchair next to another chair, which was attached to a metal track. She helped Ben switch chairs, and in a moment he was slowly traveling down a set of stairs on a motorized ride. It was soothing.

It was dark at the bottom of the stairs, but someone turned on a light. There was another wheelchair there, too, but Ben was tired of wheelchairs so he stood up and walked. It was a big room with a fat bed and a desk and a computer with a big screen and a TV and a big glass box with fish inside. "What?" he asked, pointing to it.

"Aquarium," the man said. "Your fish have missed you. We lost Minerva, unfortunately. But look, Pedro Escobar is there, and he's waving his whiskers at you."

Ben stared back and wrinkled his mouth at the fish.

Ariela was crying. He stared at her too, but she only cried more.

He sat on the bed. It was soft and springy. It was the best thing he had felt in a long time. It smelled nice, too. This was a much nicer place than the hospital. "Soft," he said. "Nice."

"Yes," the woman said.

"You like it?" the man asked.

Ben lay back. Someone had painted stars on the ceiling. "Sky," he said.

He felt his eyes growing heavy. He was beginning to sleep. But then someone began to talk to him, right in his ear.

"It is the early autumn sky, western hemisphere," the voice said. "You can see Orion's Belt in the lower portion. The stars are phosphorescent, so you get the full impact when the lights are off. We can turn the lights off and you'll see."

Ben opened his eyes. A teenager was standing next to his bed. Ben examined his face. He had seen the face before. He was happy to see the face.

"I think he wants to sleep, honey," said the woman.

Ben took the boy's hand and smiled. The boy's hand was warm. He wasn't smiling. In the pictures he was never smiling either. Everybody in the pictures looked like a TV character, but the boy did not. The boy was inside. He was inside Ben.

"Chris," Ben said.

29

August 10

"He only knew who Chris was," Ariela said as she yanked the steering wheel onto Spruce Street, where Niko lived. "Not me, not you, not his own mother and father. Only his brother who, and I know I'll rot in hell for saying this, doesn't feel a thing about him."

She pulled to a stop in front of Niko's house. He was still collecting his thoughts after the party. He knew Ariela had stayed up troubleshooting the dance company's website for the third straight night. She had been complaining of insomnia and anxiety for weeks, and she hadn't stopped crying the whole time she was in Ben's house, so Niko knew not to take everything she said tonight at face value. Still, he wasn't exactly in peak Ariela-maintenance mode right now. "You can't say Chris doesn't feel a thing. That's cruel."

"I know. I'm sorry. But clinically speaking—"

"Chris wrote a poem about Ben."

"A sestina. Months in the making. With Excel. Ode on a Spreadsheet."

"You don't write poems with that much dedication and passion if you don't feel anything."

"How do we know it's not just a group of numbers that mean nothing to anyone but Chris?" She flung her head back against the driver's seat headrest and groaned at the car ceiling. "Listen to me! What have I become? I am a monster. Please put me under the car."

"Will you stop?" Niko said. "This is not about you. And you may think all this crypto-ironic-suicidal crap is funny, but I don't, and when I hear it coming from your mouth, it just makes me want to call nine one one."

"I'm not serious, Niko."

"Well, I am," Niko shot back. "I'm the one who has been here all year. I'm the one who's been talking to Ben's parents, one at a time, passing messages between them, repeating the same stuff over and over. When they're away, I'm the one who drives to Chris's school if something goes wrong. I mow the lawn and shovel the walk, I make sure the timers are working and no one's broken in to steal the silverware."

"Well, you marry him, then, if you're so dedicated!" Ariela got out of the car, slammed the door, and began walking down the block.

Niko climbed out the passenger side. "Where are you going? It's your car!"

"For a walk," she shouted back. "With the hope that you won't be here when I get back."

"I live here!" He ran after her and tried to turn her around, but she spun back. "Ariela, I'm sorry. Here I am saying 'it's not about you' and then going all martyr on you. Look, we're all kind of strung out. I know how hard this is for you. It's been a strange day. Can we have a truce?"

Ariela turned. Her eyes were red and far away. "Do you have ice cream? Or vodka?"

"We can mix them," Niko said.

"Deal." As they walked back toward his house, Ariela leaned her head against his shoulder. "I'm sorry."

"Hi, sorry. I'm Niko."

Ariela punched him in the shoulder. "Ben used to say that."

"In his rare obnoxious moments," Niko replied, "which is why I've taken to it so naturally."

They walked up the front path and Niko unlocked the door. His parents had gone directly from the Brights' house to a benefit dinner, so the place was quiet, empty, and dark.

Turning on the lights, Niko went into the kitchen. He opened the fridge and said, "There are a couple of beers."

But Ariela was already in the living room liquor closet, pouring herself a glass of Mr. Petropoulos's coveted Metaxa Five Star. "My dad will kill you," Niko said.

"No, he'll kill you," she said, coming back to the table with at least an inch of golden liquid. "I'm a girl. I don't drink."

"He measures that stuff! He notices when it evaporates."

Ariela shrugged. "Maybe he won't mind. He'll think you were manning up."

"True."

She took a slug. "Ben never liked to drink," she said. "Ben was perfect."

Above them, the fluorescent kitchen light hummed, and the refrigerator motor kicked in on a different note. Niko sounded out the two notes. "A tritone?"

"Perfect fourth," Ariela said. "Maybe a little sharp."

"'Maria,'" Niko sang. The interval between *Ma* and *ri* was a singers' mnemonic device for the dissonant sound of a tritone, exactly three whole steps.

"'Here comes the bride,'" Ariela sang in return, the jump from *here* to *comes* being a perfect fourth, *do* to *fa* in a do-re-mi scale.

Neither exactly matched the gap between the fridge and the light, but Niko liked being with someone who knew the code.

Ariela suddenly groaned and slapped her forehead. "Oh my god, did we just sing those two melodies?"

"I liked it," Niko said. "Was it good for you?"

"'Maria' and 'Here Comes the Bride'? Is this what the last few days of summer are going to be like? One big Freudian slip after the other?" She swigged the rest of her Metaxa and went back into the living room. "I need another, quick."

"Are you becoming a cliché?" Niko asked.

"No, I'm becoming a drunk," she replied sweetly, coming back into the kitchen with two full glasses. "I recommend it highly. Take. Drink."

Niko didn't like the direction of this conversation. "You seem angry."

"He's my fiancé."

"He doesn't have to be. You don't act like you want that."

Ariela drank the rest of her glass and fell silent for a few seconds. "That is so unfair, Niko. How do you know what's in my mind?"

"I don't. You never tell me."

"Why should I? Why should I have to say I love him to you? There. I love him, okay? Are those the words you wanted to hear? Those words aren't for you. They're for him and me. I've known it for as long as I can remember. I love him and I will never love anyone like that for the rest of my life. I just spent a year surrounded by some smart, kind, funny, talented, hot-looking guys and I was lonely and scared and hurting inside, and I was also five hundred and sixty-three miles away. So I could have done whatever I wanted. Even so, none of them was him. Even the best of them, even the guys that reminded me of him most, if you stacked them up side-by-side, everyone else was the CBS version. I could hear his voice talking to me, I knew what his reactions would be, I could smell him. Do you know what that feels like? No, you don't. Right now I want to be with him more than anything in the world. And it's hard for me to face something I've been denying all year long. He's not him anymore. He's gone, Niko."

"But—" Niko began.

"And don't give me your morbid little story about Uncle Petros again either, because that doesn't apply here. Ben is not dead, and he's not alive. He just isn't. Do you understand? What am I supposed to do, Niko?"

Her words were becoming crueler and crueler, and Niko was less willing to make excuses for her. She was flying out of orbit and something had to pull her back in.

He realized she had opened up to him, and he owed her no less. The events of the year tumbled around inside his head, things he had and hadn't shared with her. There was one biggie that he'd never dared to bring up.

"He got in, you know," Niko said.

Ariela stared at him blankly. "Um, translate, please."

"Ben," Niko replied. "He applied to Chase and got in."

"Is this a joke?"

"That's how much he loved you," Niko said. "He didn't tell his mom or dad. He must have paid for the app himself. He hid the acceptance letter but his mom found it. I saw it."

"If you saw it," Ariela said sharply, "what was on the envelope?"

"A thumbs-up print. In the left-hand corner."

Ariela sank. She shook her head. "He never told me."

"That's the way he was," Niko said. "Is. He wanted to be with you."

"If he wanted to be with me," Ariela said. "he wouldn't have gone off to war! Must have been a tough decision—hmm, let me see, getting shot at in the Iraqi desert . . . college with Ariela . . . getting blown up . . . college with Ariela. . . . Hey, no-brainer!"

"He was unsure. The assignment from the Army came before the acceptance, and he had no choice."

"You—you shithead!" Ariela leapt across the table and pounded Niko on the chest. "Why did you tell me this? You just want to make me miserable!"

Niko grabbed her arms. "I don't!"

"Then what are you trying to do?"

"I don't know!"

She collapsed into him, sobbing. "What are we going to do, Niko? What's going to happen to him? Why doesn't he recognize us? What's going on in his head? Will he be whole again? Will he be happy?"

Niko held her tight, rocking her back and forth. "I don't know . . . I don't know . . . "

"I feel so lonely," she said. They sat there for a long, long time, listening to the duet of the appliances. Finally Ariela lifted her face to his. "I need . . . to lie down."

He nodded. He heard her breath synchronized with his, growing quicker, as she fell asleep on his shoulder.

30

August 11

Ben couldn't sleep. People stared at him from all around the room. They were not real people. But they were laughing and smiling and making funny faces. He was among them, too. That made him feel cold and not sleepy. Why was he in those pictures?

Everybody was a child. Women were girls and men were boys. Ben was a man, so he must have been a boy.

Men remembered when they were boys. Dr. Larsen talked about this. He was born in a place called Båstad. It sounded funny, halfway between "Bostad" and "Boostad." Dr. Larsen didn't remember being born, but he did remember being little and running around with no shoes and going to a place called Mellbystrand in the summer and stepping on a piece of broken glass and watching a doctor stitch him up and then he knew he wanted to be a doctor when he was big.

Did you have to remember what you wanted to be when you were big, back when you were little? What if you didn't? Did that mean you couldn't be anything?

Ben thought about a movie he saw, where people's brains were invaded. They couldn't think or talk. What if they took your memory but left everything else? What if they took your memory first, and then the other things? What if they were here in the room, waiting for you to go to sleep?

What if they were hiding behind the table full of pictures?

"Go away!" His arm could make them go away. He lashed out with it. There was a noise that hurt his ears. And then the table was empty and he felt much, much better.

"Ben?"

Ben stopped breathing for a moment. But he knew whose voice it was. A light went on overhead and the woman who was his mother appeared at the top of the stairs. She had on a thick robe and was tying it with a belt.

He wanted to stand up but when he moved his foot he stepped on something that gave him pain.

"What were you shouting about?" She was walking down the stairs now. His toes felt warm, and he looked down to see that they were in a pool of blood. "What was that crashing noise? Oh my god, what did you do?"

Now she was turning around and shouting "Frank." Very loud. That was the man's name.

Ben watched her pick up the pictures that were on the floor. Some of them were made of glass and they were broken. The ones that were on the table.

Who put them on the floor?

Who else was down here?

The woman was now touching his foot. It hurt! Who was she? What was she doing?

Why was he here?

He didn't like it here. He wanted to be back with Dr. Larsen.

"Ben? Are you all right?" the woman was asking.

Now the man was running down the stairs. He was using a loud voice.

Ben lay back on the bed. He closed his eyes and called as loud as he could. "Help . . . me!"

31

November 25

"You are looking fine, young man," said Hayseed. "Wish I could walk as good as you. Hey, you still sing?"

"Row, row, row your boat," Ben warbled.

Hayseed let out a loud whoop that made the cashier look. "This guy has not changed a bit!" he announced.

Hayseed's real name was Wade. He had been in Iraq, where they had been friends. Now he was visiting for two days, and Ben's mother loved him. He always said everything was perfect, he gave toasts at every meal with funny jokes, he washed dishes, and he always asked if he could help. He was a gentleman. He talked funny, a little bit like Jed Clampett on TV. When Ben had told him that, Hayseed had burst out laughing and said that Ben had "not changed a bit." He said that a lot. It felt nice.

Now they were in the Waldbaum's supermarket together. Hayseed had only one leg, but with his crutches he moved very fast. Ben moved slowly. He was pushing the cart. Ben's father was waiting out in the minivan, because Hayseed had insisted that he and Ben go into the store together.

"I'm supposed to ask if you remember what's on the list," Hayseed said. "It's a mnemonic. A memory kind of thing."

Ben stopped walking and thought carefully. "Milk. Tea. Chicken legs. Spaghetti. Mustard . . . "

"And . . . ?" Hayseed said.

"Um . . . " Ben thought: *You put milk in tea, you put chicken on top of spaghetti, you put mustard on . . .* "Hot dogs."

"Yee-hah!" Hayseed shouted. "Okay, lieutenant, what shall I procure?"

"Milk. Against back wall," Ben said.

"Which part? It's a big wall, soldier."

Ben imagined the back wall. The milk was at the end of this aisle and just to the left. Hayseed was already hopping away. His shoulders were broad. He was wearing his uniform, crutches tucked under his arm.

A mom wheeled a cart by him, with a little boy in the seat. He was fidgeting and squalling. A red doll fell out of the cart, but the mom didn't see it. She just grabbed a can of tomato sauce and kept walking. No one noticed the doll.

"Ten o'clock . . . ," Ben said.

"Copy," Hayseed called over his shoulder.

Ten o'clock, upper-left side of the clock, nine to the left, six behind you, three to the right, twelve straight ahead. Eyes moving. Eyes hurting. Heat. Scratchy throat.

"Window," Ben said. "Second floor."

"What?" Hayseed replied.

The doll was growing larger.

"Move, move, move!" Ben shouted. His throat was closing up. He was hot. The equipment was loading his shoulder down.

"I'm tryin'!" Hayseed replied.

Ben felt his breath quickening. Someone was running from window to window. He was carrying a rifle.

"Moving below!"

Hayseed was out of sight. Ben pulled the metal cart in front of him and dropped to the ground. He braced himself for the big noise, but it didn't come. Someone was laughing. They were laughing at them.

"Ajji ajji ajji hajj hajji . . . "

Someone was coming out of the house. He was dressed in white. He had blood on his shirt. Something in his hand.

A cell phone.

Ben's eyes widened. The doll was glowing bright. The doll was on fire.

Ben turned and ran. He screamed. No one was moving. Everyone was going to die. He tripped, and things fell all around him. They were throwing tuna fish cans now. To slow them down. Where was Hayseed? Other people were running toward him. To attack him. They were surrounding him. They looked mad and scared. One of them was holding a cell phone. "The toy!" Ben shouted. "The toy!"

He looked back to the little red blob on the floor.

Tickle Me Elmo sat up and laughed.

32

November 25

"Is he awake?" Hayseed asked.

Ben opened his eyes. He was in his room again. He saw Orion's Belt. His mom and dad were hovering over him, as well as Ariela and Chris. Hayseed raised his eyebrows and smiled. "Well, good morning, Private. Welcome to La La Land."

"I had. Dream. Very bad," Ben said.

"The people at Waldbaum's had a worse one," Hayseed said. "You messed up the store pretty good."

"Um, we weren't going to talk about that," Ariela said.

Hayseed shrugged. "Hell, I was proud of him."

"My arm hurts," Ben said. He looked down and saw bruises up and down his left arm.

"You had a flashback or something," Ariela said, taking his hand. "But you're okay now."

"Sounded like you were back in Iraq," Hayseed said.

Ben's heart started beating. Everyone was talking at once. He tried to sit up, but Ariela was gently pushing him back into bed. His father was talking with Hayseed, telling him they needed to go upstairs to have a talk. Soon they were going upstairs, and so was his mom. Only Ariela and Chris remained. Chris had been sitting far away, so quiet that Ben hadn't noticed him.

"What happened?" Ben asked.

Ariela knelt close to him. "I'm not sure if it's good to talk about what just happened."

"I saw things," Ben said.

"You should rest," Ariela replied.

"Hayseed is missing a leg," Ben said.

"Yes, he is," Ariela said. "Please. Sleep."

"He's my friend. I knew him."

Ariela shuddered. Her voice got very low. "Ben, are you remembering things?"

"I remember. Elmo. Elmo was in the store." Now he was shaking too.

"The doll," Ariela said. "They found a doll on the floor in Waldbaum's, yes."

"It's bad," Ben said. "It's going to . . . "

His mind saw a big, yellow village and people in white, then it saw nothing.

"Going to what?" Ariela said.

He didn't want to answer. He didn't answer.

"Do you remember anything good, Ben?" Ariela said. "From before?"

"No. Yes."

"Chris, please come here," Ariela said.

Chris stood stiffly from his chair. He was carrying a manila envelope. He knelt down next to Ben and put the envelope on his bed.

Ariela put her arm around him. "Chris, please sit still with me. I know you don't feel right, but you're safe. Ben is going to look at you, okay?" She turned to Ben and said, "Would you please look at your brother? You don't have to say anything. Just look at him."

"Okay," Ben said. "Hi."

"I wrote something," Chris said. "It's in that envelope on the bed."

"What is it?" Ben asked.

"A poem," said Chris. "I wrote it by hand."

"He wrote it last year," Ariela said. "But he didn't show it to anybody. He didn't want to. He wants to now."

"I started writing it when you were in Washington," Chris said. "In Walter Reed Army Medical Center."

"I don't remember," Ben said.

"You were in a coma," Chris replied.

Ariela held the sheet out to Ben. "Why don't you read it?"

"Did you? Read it?" Ben asked.

"None of us have," she replied.

Ben tore open the envelope and pulled out a sheet of paper. "I used the VLOOKUP formula," Chris said.

Ben held the sheet into the light and read:

My Brother
A Sestina
By Christopher Ian Bright

We visit Ben whenever we please
(At least we think it's Ben!)
I say, "My name is Chris."

So many miles we have come
in order for him to hear
us, to bring his memory back

Week Two: We go back
with a radio to please
my brother. He can hear,
so I say, "Hi, Ben!
"When we go, you'll come?
"This is your brother Chris!"

Third week for Chris.
Mom rubs Ben's back.
But Ariela can't come,
although I begged, "Please!"
Don't worry, okay, Ben?
(Do you really hear?)

Hey, I hear
you said "Chris"!!!
You see, Ben,
you're coming back!
So hurry, please,
hurry and come!

I'll come.
I'll hear.
So please,
tell Chris!

Talk back
now, Ben.

Ben,
come
back.
Hear
Chris,
please.

Ben, hear?
Come, Chris.
Back, please!

© by Christopher Ian Bright.

Ben looked at Chris, and then he looked at the poem again. "I love this," he said.

"Chris, this is beautiful," Ariela said.

"I'm writing a pantoum about baseball," Chris said. "About the history of the slugging percentage."

"Really?" Ben said. "I would like to read it. This makes me feel. Proud."

"Proud?" Ariela said.

Ben nodded. Pride was a thing Dr. Larsen talked about a lot. Being proud. He said it wasn't something you knew, it was something you felt.

He felt.

Ariela leaned closer. "When you first came home in August,

Ben, you said his name. You said 'Chris.' No one was telling you what to say."

Ben nodded. "Yes."

"You remembered him."

"Yes."

"But you haven't been remembering other people. Not really."

He looked at her. He didn't know whether to say yes or no.

"How much do you remember about Chris?" Ariela continued. "Should I tell you stories about him, about stuff you and he did together?"

"No stories," Ben said.

"We can talk about the nineteen eighty-six championship Mets," Chris said. "You made a YouTube video setting the Bill Buckner first-base bobble to music, and I have seen it seven hundred and twenty-six times."

"Chris, can you stay quiet for . . ."—she looked at her watch—". . . five minutes, and let your brother just look at you?"

Chris sat silently, which she took for a yes.

"Can you do that, Ben?" Ariela asked.

"Yes."

Ben looked at his brother but Chris's face got all unfocused. He blinked and he was in focus again. Ariela wiped something from his cheek. "Breathe and look, Ben. Breathe and look."

Ben blinked. He blinked again. He was seeing a baby. He was kissing that baby and playing with it. He was watching two grownups fight, and the baby was in the hospital and Ben was visiting. He was worried. He saw a dark spot on a wall, a crack. It was blood. A line of blood that went almost to the floor. He blinked again and Chris was staring at him and then suddenly Chris was skinnier and younger, and a great big bump had grown on his head. He kept blinking and saw Chris in a group of older people. And Chris wasn't exactly happy but everyone else was, and not-exactly-happy Chris was working hard and writing his alphabet and sometimes making a sharp sound that was a laugh, and Ben felt relief because somehow he knew Chris would no longer have so many bumps on the head. It was a great, lucky thing to live in a place where strange and smart people cared about Chris. And then he blinked one too many times and he was thinking about boots and guns and people dressed in sheets, so he stopped blinking and thinking.

Chris was still there. He had never left.

"Are you okay, Ben?" Ariela was asking.

"Meat locker," Chris said. "Locked door. A cleaver, a toaster oven, a light saber, and a carton of milk. Eli Manning and Genghis Kahn. Who lives?"

The window was opening and the sun was in Ben's eyes but it didn't feel hot and it didn't feel sandy. It felt warm and good. "Eli," he said.

Chris raised his hand. "You will regret this."

"Three," Ben said, "two."

"Da man," Chris said.

Ben slapped Chris's hand. "Da man, brother."

Ariela was crying again. She loved to cry. She put her arm around Chris, but he shook it off.

Ben stared at her, too. Her eyes were glassy. Her hair fell forward in curls. He touched her hair.

"Ben?" Ariela said.

Her hair was soft and almost white in the lights behind her that flickered and brightened and oozed like blood. He forced himself to breathe and look, breathe and look . . .

"Hey, are you okay?" Ariela asked. "I don't mean to upset you. If you're tired, I'll leave you alone."

. . . And the ooze became circles of blue and yellow, purple and red, receding and brightening while the basement walls faded to black and reached back into the universe . . .

" . . . I'll be here for a couple more days before school starts again . . . "

She was rising now, her mouth moving, neck softly sinewed, eyes pulling him upward . . .

"Niko sends his best, but he just started his freshman year at Pomona and the trip is too expensive so he'll see you at Christmas . . ."

. . . Until he too was lifted from the bed and they were flying together, weightless on a column of breath. They were released from the world, from sand and rucksacks, radios and red dolls, the suck unembraced, they were going to a new place, and nothing could touch them now.

"Maria," he said.

Ariela smiled. And then she laughed. And she said his name. And he knew it was his name.

Ben.

His name was Ben.

St. Sebastian's Catholic School
London, Ontario